SW

The sensu... ...ctorian maid

Also available

Sweet Fanny

Sweet Fanny's Diary

edited and illustrated by

Faye Rossignol

HEADLINE

ISBN 0 7472 3298 9

Printed and bound in Great Britain by
Collins, Glasgow

HEADLINE BOOK PUBLISHING PLC
Headline House
79 Great Titchfield Street
London W1P 7FN

Sweet Fanny's Diary

[Fanny's diary begins with a draft of a letter to her grandmother, the Countess de C., who had arranged for her to travel to France and be seduced by the Count's son (her stepson) François.]

PARIS
Monday, 19th August 1850

Dear Countess,
I wish you had let me call you grandmother, though I understand why a woman as young as you, and who looks even younger, would be reluctant to accept that venerable title. But 'Countess' does seem so formal; and it does not sit well with the things I now have to tell you!

Well, what am I to say? What could possibly excuse my appalling behaviour these last two weeks? When I left Victoria on the Dover train, I promise you, I fully intended to follow your plan. I was to meet your footman at Calais and be escorted to Paris, where you would prepare me to lose my virginity to Comte François. And then, when he had completed my Sentimental Education, we would see whether the life of a Lady of Pleasure would suit me ... and so on.

Oh, dearest sweetest Countess, you have never shown me anything but kindness, and I did so want to please you – quite apart from the enormous honour and the equally boundless pleasure I would have felt in being seduced by a lover of Comte François' distinction. But there you have it, you see! For, whatever might have passed between him and me, it would not have been a *seduction*. Your letters had so inflamed me that I should have gone willingly to his bed, tearing the clothes off my

1

own back in my haste to be under him at last. And then I think I should have missed the greatest pleasure a young girl may experience in affairs of this kind: the pleasure of being seduced.

What do I know about such things, I hear you ask? Oh, my dear Countess – I think I know everything! Let me tell you the way it happened. I assure you now: I believe there never was a seduction quite like mine since civilization began!

The moment we got aboard the ferry steamer, I made for that bit of deck in the front which rises toward the bowsprit; Mason, my mother's footman, who was escorting me, said there was less chance of being assailed by smuts there. It wasn't long before I was joined by a dashing young officer in the French dragoons – that is, we stood about eight paces apart, and the curve of the rail meant he was facing three quarters away from me. I could see almost nothing of his features and yet I couldn't take my eyes off him – though my glance was sidelong, so no one who saw me could guess where my attention was fastened. Even to look at him gave me that melting feeling between my thighs which I am sure, dear Countess, I need not describe to *you!* (However, lest you should think that was unusual, I have to confess, dear Countess, that, since reading of your triumphs in the affairs of Venus, I have had that same feeling with several other men – and nothing ever came of it. So it did not mean that what followed on this occasion was in any way inevitable. I merely report that I felt that certain thrill about him, like a warm, glowing snake inside me.)

Mason certainly didn't realize what was happening to me; he is of that cloddish breed that would rather down a pint of ale than the most willing wench in the world. So I praised him for the care he'd taken of me so far, pointed out that no harm could now befall me, here on the open deck, in full view of the captain and a couple of dozen eminently respectable-looking passengers, and with the calmest of seas ... so why didn't he relax with a reviving drink or two? Or three.

My dragoon heard all this – *he* caught the tone in my voice, even if Mason was too stupid. I could tell it from a special kind of tenseness in the way he held his shoulders when we were once again alone. I'm sure you've also felt that instantaneous kind of *rapport* with a man; there's no describing it to those who haven't, but you will understand the extraordinary power of attraction I now felt flowing between us.

Over the next fifteen minutes or so, if anyone came and stood at the rail between us, he did not move; he did not even appear to notice them. But if anyone came and stood at the rail beyond him, even though they allowed a good space between them and him, he would politely yield an inch or two – thus, quite casually and accidentally, bringing us closer together. How thrilling it was! And he knew it, too. He knew I would be at screaming point when he finally murmured, 'You are perhaps going to Paris, mam'selle?' He was still, to all the world, staring intently at the sea, taking no apparent notice of me whatever.

His voice was gentle, like a caress, yet his tone demanded an answer. 'You are impertinent, sir,' I told him. We spoke in French; no doubt he thought that would put me at a disadvantage.

'It is at once the gayest and most dangerous city in the world,' he said – as if I had replied in the warmest tones of encouragement. My heart was jumping around inside me like a fighting rabbit and I think if he had so much as touched me then I should have passed out.

'Really?' I said frostily.

'Especially for a young woman as ravishingly beautiful as yourself.'

'But most of all,' I began – and then I had to pause and swallow three times to restore the calm to my voice, though it had long since deserted the rest of me – 'most of all when she is accosted by frivolous young men who imagine they have Cupid in their pocket.'

'Ah! You suppose me the merest flatterer. How may I convince you otherwise? Shall I describe your beauty to you, mam'selle? Feature by feature?'

I made no reply.

'Remember,' he added, 'I have glanced at you but once, and now I dare not look again. For even that glimpse has pierced me to the very heart.'

'Is Notre Dame open throughout the year, pray?' I asked him. 'My aunt and I were thinking of ...'

'Your hair,' he went on, as if I were not speaking, 'is the nearest thing to gold I have ever seen. It looks pretty enough, disciplined like that into a neat bun, but when you let it down at night, it's like a cascade of blossom. Your eyes are truly extraordinary, though. On a photograph they look merely beautiful, but when one meets you in the flesh and has the opportunity to stare into them, one sees something haunting, disturbing – almost mocking – deep inside them. You are not one of those girls one forgets inside a couple of weeks. Your nose is, as yet, your weakest feature – but that's because of your age. What are you? Sixteen? Already most women would give their eye teeth to be blessed with a nose like yours. But you wait until you're twenty-one – they'll *kill* you for it then!'

He paused and stared out to sea. I knew he wanted me to press him to continue with this *catalogue raisonné*. Instead, I took out my little notebook and began, ostentatiously, to tot up the expenses of the journey so far. I made the same addition five times, and got five different answers. But that was because I was really listening to him. Anyway, I took an average of the five answers; that's how I do most of my sums.

'Your lips,' he went on when he realized I was not going to encourage him openly, 'show what a contradiction you are. The upper one is so firm and chaste. It promises love ... but at some infinitely delayed moment in your life. Yet look at the lower one! Did you ever see anything so generous and impulsive? I think you must be at constant war with yourself, mam'selle. One half of you says that a pleasure postponed is a pleasure sweetened. The other half says, "I want it now!" And the rest of your charms certainly do not make that battle any easier to resolve.'

Again he paused, and this time I knew he would never start again without some kind of prompting from me. 'It's a long way to France,' I mused. 'It might help pass the time, I suppose.' I did not say *what*. I simply spoke aloud, to the gulls, or anything else that might happen to overhear me.

'Your body already has that form which drives men to distraction,' he went on in that same calm voice – which was driving *me* to distraction. 'Your skin is pale bronze, half way between the untouchable milk-white of the ice-maiden and the all-too rudely touchable tan of the field girl; you provoke with the invincible purity of the one, coupled with the unrestrained availability of the other.'

There was a further silence.

'Is that all?' I asked the waves scornfully.

'I speak as I find.' For the first time I heard a smile in his tone. 'And though there is plenty more to be found, *I* have not yet been so honoured.'

The stress was odd, as if he were suggesting that others had. He must have heard the implication, too, the moment his words were out, for he now added, 'And nor, I think, has anyone else. What a privilege!'

'Privilege,' I echoed, not knowing what else to say.

5

His eyes were having the most hypnotic effect on me.

'Yes,' he asserted. *'Your* privilege! You enjoy the greatest prerogative on earth, mam'selle: the gift of your virginity. The female human form is the nearest thing we know to a proof of the existence of God. And to whom shall fall that honour, eh? Shall it be some crapulous old toad who can give you position and title? Or will you bestow that infinite blessing on some ardent young man with the stars in his hair?'

He sauntered away as if he had been a guide on a conducted tour that had reached its appointed finish. And there was his supreme cleverness, you see. He knew – with a certainty that must have been absolute – he knew that come all the saints in heaven against me, I should find some way to grant him the Favour he so ardently craved. And so eloquently, too. And yet he left me with the thought that the choice was freely mine; it was in my absolute power to say yes or no. Until then I thought his memory for my appearance to be the most perceptive thing about him – especially as he had, indeed, merely glanced at me. But now I realized that, in that glance, he must also have peered into my very soul. Somehow he had divined my one great weakness: I need to believe that the choice in these matters is mine alone. Then I am putty in their hands! How did he understand that within moments of our first meeting?

The next part you know. I gave Mason the slip at Calais and your own footman walked right past me without a sign of recognition. True, he only had my photograph to go by. And for some reason I was limping heavily by then, and my face was somehow all twisted …

Imagine my chagrin, however, when, though I had managed to secure an entire *wagon* to myself, the train pulled out of the station and no dashing young dragoon had joined me. But then, before we had even passed the first bridge down the line, the window darkened – and there he was, hanging from the carriage roof! I drew down the window and he swung lithely inwards, a shower of blue and gold, like Zeus to Danaë in her tower. The next stop was not until Amiens, so we had the carriage to ourselves for over half an hour. We wasted no time on words. I did not even ask his name, nor he mine.

I remember your description, Countess, of how the Comte took such care over your seduction – three or four days was it not, beginning in Dover and reaching its consummation at the Château? Perhaps a small part of me now regrets that my own First Time was not as leisurely; but the rest of me rejoices – for how else would I have discovered something so important about myself as I did in that half hour of sheer frenzy?

First I will tell you what he did – and you will think him a brute. Then I will tell you what I felt – and you will be sure he belongs among the stars.

He knelt before me and threw up my skirts. Then he pushed my thighs apart and took out his organ, which was stiff as iron and throbbing and hot. The gleaming, scarlet knob of it was still half shrouded in its foreskin. Remember, I had never seen this part of a man before, but without thought I took it in my hands and peeled the skin right back. He let out a great sigh and pulled me towards him. And in that same smooth action he went deep inside me. I must have been very wet already, for I felt not a thing. And then, instead of moving in and out, as I expected, he simply froze! He closed his eyes and clenched his fists and he shouted 'No!' in a despairing sort of tone. He cried again: 'No! Please no!' And then I understood he was in his *plaisir d'amour*. How did I know that? I can't explain it; I just knew it. And then I felt his gristle explode inside me there. It was like a repeating pistol, shooting again and again.

Now let me tell you what I felt. The moment that first shot hit me I had a kind of picture of what it was like inside me there; somehow I could see all four sides of my *vagin* clenched around that fat, throbbing rod of hardened flesh – and the end of me pressed against its knob – and the spouting pressure of his semen. And I honestly thought I was having a heart attack. I felt ill ... dying. I thought my heart had stopped. I couldn't breathe. I wanted to be sick. And I just collapsed against him until I felt better – which happened amazingly quickly.

And then when I glanced at him I saw an entirely new light in his eyes, a sort of wonder that grew and grew until it turned to adulation. 'You *did!*' he murmured.

At that I understood I had just had my first real *plaisir*. Oh Countess, it was nothing like those little thrills that we young girls can induce in our *petits amours* with our own fingers; this had been a brush with death itself.

Do you think it should have been more obviously thrilling? All I know is that I could not wait for it to happen again, right that minute. And, since he was still hard as a rock, and still inside me, it took only the smallest movement on my part to persuade him.

And then it was as if that first climax had unlocked a door to a new room inside me, which I could now enter and leave as often as I pleased. I could have climax after climax, entirely at will. And I'm afraid that between there and Amiens, I simply used him as a handle to that door ... oh God, I lost count of the number of times! And he, poor man, having shot his bolt so thoroughly, was unable to get there again – though he said he didn't mind ... and anyway, there'd be time enough in Paris that night.

The astonishing thing is that these other *plaisirs* were, objectively, just like the first. They tore me apart, they stopped my heartbeat, they turned my stomach to jelly … and yet now the thrill of them was every bit as great as I had always expected. How can I account for so great a difference? I remember once, at home, thinking there was a dreadful smell about; but when I commented on it, Mother said, 'But darling, that is the cheese you asked me to get in especially for you.' And suddenly that smell – though quite obviously the identical smell as before – became the most marvellous aroma. That's a feeble sort of way of explaining how that first experience of sexual climax, though identical with all the others, could yet be so different.

A young couple got in at Amiens and by the look of them they'd rather be doing what we had just done all the way from Calais. But Carlos and I (oh yes, I had learned his name by now!) just sat and stared at each other in wonder all the rest of the way. Most of my wonder, I must confess, was at myself. Do you not think it extraordinary, Countess, that I should have taken to pleasuring so immediately and so absolutely? I mean, without any preparation at all? True, your letters to me over the last few months were so vivid that I could be forgiven for thinking I had already been pleasured countless times before I even set foot in France; but that sort of book-wisdom has deserted many a beginner on the night when the curtain finally rises. But from everything you have said – and from those books you sent me – it is quite clear that a woman needs a certain preparatory stimulation before she can rise to her *plaisir*. There is a whole ritual of loving and tenderness to ease its way. But there was I, *virgo intacta* one moment and in the next I found myself in the throes of a climax so mighty I confused it with dying! Carlos had not touched me anywhere else, not with his hands nor his lips nor his tongue; he had not caressed my hair nor whispered my name.

I believe this deflowering was sent to me as an omen. That First Time is so all-important to a girl, for it sets the pattern for the rest of her amatory life. I don't mean it in the crude sense that from now on I shall be seeking out men who can give me lightning orgasms! (Dear me, no – and I shall tell you why in a moment.) But it revealed to me that I am a particular kind of woman – that I was born to give and take that pleasure with men – and that is bound to point me in certain directions and steer me away from others.

What's this, you ask? Was it not exactly the same for you, although your seduction lasted as many days as mine did seconds? Very well, I concede all that. We are both princesses of the Realm of Pleasure; you woke up to it, slowly, luxuriously, stretching yourself particle by particle until at last you sat up and looked around and realized you were there. I died on the road to my own Damascus and fell through the sky – to land, by great good fortune, in the very heart of it.

But these comparisons are idle. We are all unique. I make no likeness or contrast between us when I add this: Because I know I can open the door to that room at any time, I find an enormous pleasure in saying, 'No! Leave it closed for a while.' I anticipate my story slightly, but I must explain this. The sweetest delight and joy, for me, is to deny my lover when he is ardent. My insides may be melting, I may feel hollow and sick with my lust for him, he may brandish his weapon before me, hot and ready, to show me how his desire for me is now aflame ... and every atom of me may be whispering yes, yes, yes – and yet I hear my voice say no, I see my hand push him away, I rebound in amazement as my feet carry me from him. All this is only to tease him, of course. He knows it is a game I play to inflame us both still further – and yet I play it so convincingly he half-believes I truly mean it.

And believe me, dear Countess, I am so lost in the pleasuring of my *vagin* that, without the absolute certainty I gained, a mile south of Calais and an inch south of my navel, I should never have the courage to do it at all.

But wait a minute! I have just read back over those last few paragraphs, feeling I had missed something – and, indeed, I had! For now I realize that my wishing *yes* and saying *no* is part and parcel of my general character. I adore chocolate, for instance; I live for the taste of it; I always have a piece or two in my pocket book or bag. Yet nine times out of ten, my hand will steal towards it, and I will simply tell myself *no*. And then – oh! the pleasure when I finally disobey myself! There is a value, you see – a measure of self-education – in writing these things down. Perhaps I shall, after all, keep a diary as you suggested.

Anyway, let me tell you of the events whose conclusion I have just anticipated. It began with our arrival in Paris. I thought he might have to join his regiment, or at least report to his colonel; but no, he took me directly to a little hotel in one of those squares on the southern slopes of the hill of Montmartre; that old windmill was at the bottom of the garden. Having been so hasty on the train, perhaps he now thought it prudent to borrow some of my capacity for postponement. We lingered for ever over our evening meal, knowing that an infinity of joyous hours stretched ahead of us. I teased myself, imagining him sitting there without the protection of that gorgeous uniform; then I'd see the cheeky red knob of his pego sticking up above the edge of the tablecloth, its one eye fixed on me, begging ... pleading. And that would only make me smile, because I knew that before the night was out, it would be begging ... pleading to be allowed to stop and get some rest! I was wet halfway down my thighs by the time we finally tripped upstairs to our room.

There, remembering one of your letters to me, I asked him if he wished to do something that would please me more than anything else in the world. Of course, he was only too delighted. So I asked him to undress me slowly, exploring each revelation of my body and telling me what feelings it gave him. I didn't add that I wanted to lie completely naked on him, while he was still in full uniform, and pleasure myself, but that was my intention.

It didn't work out like that, though, for his skill at undressing me and his hypnotic voice telling me of all my charms and how I would drive men mad and so on ... well, it undid me completely. I lay there in a frenzy of delight in which everything female and gorgeous and warm in the entire cosmos suddenly found its centre in me. And that loneliness which each of us carries within ourselves (and which, indeed, we call our 'self') was suddenly lifted from me. And the real me – something far deeper than my self – was liberated, free to expand. I just seemed to flow out and join up with all those other female ... things – spirits, forces – I don't know what to call them. And then I knew that to *be* female was the greatest privilege in the universe. And to yield up my femininity to these ecstasies was its greatest bounty and delight.

I could go on to tell you we enjoyed each other in this position or that – and I'm sure I'd be right, for I know we passed through the entire gymnasium of loving attitudes. I could add that for the past five days we have done little else but add to each other's pleasures, or recover from them, or anticipate their next flowering. But all of that would miss the point – which is that I believe all you hoped to accomplish with me has now been accomplished. I am now as dedicated to the pursuit of that sweet pleasuring which flows into and out of my well of delight as you could possibly have desired – but perhaps not in quite the way you might have wished for me. If so, then I believe your hopes were always forlorn. I could never be a Lady of Pleasure in the sense that I might hire my passions to half a dozen Lovers each day or night. My ecstasy lies as much in denial as in yielding. I must be wooed gently into the trap of a man's embrace – even when I think I might die of chagrin if I evaded it! If I ever barter my favours for gold (as I expect I shall have to or how may I live?), then it must be to one lover at a time, and that time to endure a month or a year. I am a courtesan, *une grande horizontale.* Your livelier ways are not for me, and I believe my spirit has inclined that way from birth.

I do not say I achieved all this by myself, not even if I add the enormous help of my own sweet Carlos. I think the greater part of the achievement, such as it is, is yours, dear Countess. In the letters you wrote me (whose publication you are even now, I trust, negotiating with Mr Raines) you allowed me – nay, you *challenged* me – to explore my sexual nature in the safe seclusion of my own locked bedroom; to which challenge I most obediently and gleefully rose! I had travelled nine tenths the journey to this my present understanding before I even set out for France; who else may I thank for that but you?

So do not worry for me, my dear friend and mentor. I live now in the hope that we may meet in amity, when you may quiz me as close as you will and I shall attempt to explain it all, ten thousand times better than here.

etc.

[Here Fanny adds three afterthoughts to her draft.]

Work this in earlier somewhere:

Naturally one of my first questions to Carlos was whether he made a habit of seducing innocent maidens on the English Channel like that. He said he had never before taken a girl's virginity in such a hasty fashion; indeed, he had never before done it inside three days, except with very common girls in the fields. Nor had he ever presumed to speak to any woman as he had spoken to me when we stood by the rail of that boat. But some powerful force of absolute assurance had moved him to it then – but only because it was *me*. And once he had started, and realized that I was responding, notwithstanding my outward coolness, he saw no cause to stop. (Then he rather spoiled this assertion by saying that he had once enjoyed a girl – a total stranger – who was standing between her mother and her father at a horse race in the Bois de Boulogne – in a very dense crowd, to be sure. But, he added, she had been no virgin, which he had sensed the moment he raised her skirt from behind and she cooperated in every way.)

I did not describe Carlos:

He is not tall and not especially handsome – except that a uniform always does marvels for a man, as you well know. He is not fat, but he has a little round pot of a belly, which is actually all muscle. He is very stocky and muscular all over. He has beautiful, sensitive eyes and the most expressive lips, which can plead, laugh, and make you shiver with their severity, one after another. If I close my eyes I see him in a pose that, for some reason, is the epitome of him: standing before me, stark naked, with the whorls of black hair like decorations all over him – circles round his nipples, a river down round his navel to that tangled forest around the hardest, cheekiest, dearest tool you ever saw (or *I* ever saw). I see it hot and hard, still slightly dripping with semen from our previous pleasuring, but ready again – which is why he's wearing that wicked grin, of course. And I'm wondering is he going to flow over me gently, like a mid-ocean wave, or is he going to rush upon me like a mad bull of a man? – of both of which he is quite capable.

I do not think I love him, but, oh, I have needed his skills this week gone by!

Also thank her for the lovely silver douche for 'washing the babies out.' Carlos was fascinated by its construction – a long, thin male organ with the douche water in rubber testicles. He loves using it on me after our frequent pleasures.

[The draft of the letter ends at that. Fanny's first diary entry follows on the same page.]

Oh, my dear, sweet, wise grandmama – shall I ever have the courage to send you that letter? Will you not sense at once all the things my pride has forced me to omit? I think you will. Then you will set your hounds to sniff me out, which will not be difficult, considering that my only commodity now is my body. And then I shall be brought home in ignominy.

Well, I shall resist it as long as possible. What else can I do? Since my sweet Carlos borrowed all my money, and is now arrested and likely to be shot as a deserter and impostor (for he was never above a corporal in his life), what else can I do?

On our final night together, when he confessed all the trouble he was having with his many bankers and his father's lawyers and his vast estates ... and I suddenly realized what sort of a man he truly was, then – just to test him – I suggested that some rich gentleman might wish to pay dearly for my Favours (hoping my Carlos would strike me to the ground, call me whore, swear he would rather sell himself than me …) and all he did was write me the address of a M Vallodon, who lives in a smart house on the Champs Élysées and who keeps a stable of courtesans of the highest class … Well, I shall go there tomorrow and we shall see how much of my pride I can swallow when I have to.

CHEZ M LE DUC DE R.
Wednesday, 21st August,
1850.

What a day! Say what you will about the Life of Pleasure, you cannot deny it is a life of constant surprise. Is it still only Wednesday? I must write it all down before I forget a thing.

Thank God we had paid the hotel in advance. I had no breakfast but at least I got a good night's sleep. (Was it odd, that untroubled sleep? Should not a young girl who had lost her virginity not a week since, and who knew she was about to sell her body into virtual slavery to any man with enough coins to rub together, should she not have fretted all night? Or awakened at least *once?* I did not. That is all I know.) I sent a message to M Vallodon early that morning, setting forth some of my difficulties (but of course not saying a word about my connection with the Count and Countess de C.) and asking for his help in securing me a *position.* He obliged me to call at two o'clock that very afternoon.

I spent my last sous in *eau de toilette,* and ribbons for my hair, and some of the daintiest underwear ever. I remembered the Countess's wisdom in this, when she told me that a Lady of Pleasure sells *nothing* – a mere hole, an emptiness surrounded by herself; therefore the adornment of that surrounding, that delicate, soft, pearly pink oyster of flesh, becomes all-important.

16

I set out at half past noon, being compelled to walk all the way from Montmartre down to the Champs Élysées, for I had not even a few sous for a cab. August is a dreadful month in Paris. The whole city seems deserted and I fell to wondering where M Vallodon might find trade enough for his regular stable, without taking one more filly onto his books – and a young, unbroken one at that. But then I supposed there must be many government functionaries and men of affairs who simply could not get away from the city but whose wives and children would see no reason to stay in the bake-oven with them. And a summer heat of that degree undoubtedly provokes our carnal desires to the point where we go mad if we refuse them a moment longer. It most certainly had that effect on me as I strolled as slowly as I dared beneath the trees. I was aware of men's eyes upon me, watching me from café terraces, looking down on me from upper balconies. Their eyes stripped me as I walked and I could feel the weight of all that desire, like hands caressing me. It would have made me breathless just to stand still, and by the time I was half-way there I was already cheerful in the knowledge that my passions would accept more men than my taste might find agreeable – which was no bad mood in which to begin my new way of life.

I wondered then what sort of interview might await me at the end of this long stroll. How many hopeful young ladies approached him every week? As few as one? Or as many as a hundred? Did he try them all? How did he judge those who might not be to his taste but who might please another man beyond measure? Whatever might be the answers to these questions, M Vallodon was obviously a man of wide and subtle experience. Was I not mad to think that I – after one short week with one sole lover – might be capable of giving pleasure to such a person? Every female wile since the invention of love had surely been turned upon him; so what hope had I, who had no wiles at all?

I was in a fair lather by the time I pulled at his bell. I think if he had answered in person, I should have dropped at his feet and begged him to take me on without trial and give me to some callow youth who would not notice all my *gaucherie*. Fortunately I was answered by a motherly old woman, a maid who had been with him for years and had seen females in every state of want and terror on that same threshold.

She immediately put an arm about me and brought me down to the kitchen, where it was cool. There she gave me a glass of cold Vichy water, which greatly steadied me once more. As I revived I asked her what form this interview might take. She smiled sadly and said she could not tell me in any detail. 'The life of a courtesan who works for M Vallodon is filled with surprises, my sweet. Some are happy, some are less agreeable, but none are dangerous or truly frightening – he is very tender with his ladies, and is thus most careful in his choice of clientèle. So, my dear, the surprise of the interview must be maintained. But do not worry. Most ladies undergo it with ease.'

'And those who don't?' I asked.

She smiled encouragingly. 'They, too, learn an important fact about themselves – that the life of the courtesan is not for them. So do not think of it as a test which you pass or *fail*. You pass it to one decision or you pass it to another, you see? It is a chance to find out if you are this sort of woman or that. Not better or worse, just this or that. If I were emperor, every woman in Paris would be offered that choice.'

But I was not so easily pacified. I explained that I had no choice but to consider it a test, for if I failed, I would starve. 'I even had to walk here, all the way from my hotel in Montmartre.'

Her smile did not waver. 'M Vallodon will think of something. He adores all women. He lives for us. He would never turn you empty away.'

She went upstairs to see if her master was ready for me and returned with an immediate summons. My heart was leaping every way in my chest as she led me to the room where my fate was to be decided. Just before I went in she whispered to me – in a tone that suggested she was breaking with her duty as a servant, 'Remember now – they are trying to surprise you.'

I swallowed several times and went within. *They?* I had expected only one.

The room was octagonal, with long mirrors on seven of its walls. I could see myself – and the bed and the candelabra and the washstand – reflected an infinity of times in every direction. Most unnerving. Faint daylight struggled through some curtains shrouding a small lantern in the ceiling. It revealed that, if I was to have a partner for this test, he had not yet joined me.

'Bonjour mam'selle,' said a man – M Vallodon himself, I presumed. He was as yet no more than a voice, which appeared to be coming out of a cabinet full of china ornaments that was set against the only wall that did not support a mirror.

'Bonjour m'sieu,' I replied, with a dainty curtsey in the direction of the cabinet.

'Please take off all your clothes,' he went on. 'Imagine, if you will, that there is a gentleman in there with you and you are doing it to give him pleasure.'

I immediately placed 'my' imaginary gentleman there in the cabinet and undressed myself for his delectation alone. Indeed, I did not simply undress, I turned it into a dreamy kind of dance. I have always loved gymnastics and making my body do exactly what I want of it; and I believe my muscles and joints enjoy the discipline, too, for they often glow with the delight of their exhaustion.

So I did not feel at all foolish to be standing there, pretending a china cabinet was a gentleman, and taking off my clothes for its satisfaction.

When my breasts were bare I began to fondle them and caress the nipples to make them hard, but he called out, 'No, no, mam'selle, please leave that for later.'

'If there were a real gentleman in here with me, he would have responded by now,' I said.

He laughed. 'Very true. Well, let me tell you you're doing splendidly so far – but there's a long way to go yet, so don't be overconfident. You may take off your dress now.'

I bent forward to lift the hem and smooth out my beautiful silk stockings. (Silk, in that heat! I was surely mad, or desperate.) Also to let my breasts hang down enticingly. I had to make the most of them because I am still so young and they are not yet at their full growth. Then I snaked out of my dress, which fell in a sort of sighing of petticoats until it lay around my calves and ankles like whipped cream.

Then I had on only my stockings, the belt from which they were suspended, and a pair of silk drawers designed to reveal more than they could possibly conceal. All these garments were of a pale sky-blue silk, which I had never seen before that morning in Paris; the colour set off my golden skin and the pale forest on my mound to perfection. I fancied I heard a gasp of delight from the depths of the cabinet. But perhaps I only invented it in order to encourage myself.

Oh, I also had on a pair of shiny court shoes, dark blue, with a high heel and nothing at the back but a strap. Carlos had told me that a naked woman's heel is a powerful stimulant to a man since, viewed from behind, it resembles a naked breast or the rounded curve of her *derrière*. I now see that Carlos, in the pretence of adding to my sentimental education, was already training me as a whore. Anyway, I was able to put his advice to good use.

'Excellent,' my disembodied voice called out. 'You may leave on your underwear for the moment, mam'selle. Come close to the cabinet now and show me your most intimate charms.'

What instinct led me to take up a chair as I approached that voice? Perhaps there is more of the whore in me than I want to admit. But I used it to good advantage now, to show off those 'intimate charms' from every angle. Whatever reservations I may feel about my breasts, I take nothing but pride in all those folds and crevices between my thighs. Carlos swore it was the prettiest thing he had ever seen. When I lie on my back with my thighs half spread, he said, 'You can see a little bit of everything – not much but just enough to tantalize!'

'Oh, mam'selle,' came the voice from beyond. 'This grows better and better. Tell me, d'you see at the bottom of this cabinet, a pair of drawers between those wickedly suggestive cabriole legs? Please open the one on the right and take out whatever you find there.'

Now that *was* a surprise! For what I found there was a perfect replica of a man's erect organ, made in some kind of rubbery substance but with a harder core – perhaps rubber cast over ebony. And it was painted in the most perfectly natural colours, so that at first sight I was sure it was the real thing, severed and lying there. I gave a little cry of shock and I'm sure I heard laughter beyond the opaque glass at the back of that cabinet.

'Imagine you have a bowl of water there with you,' the voice went on. 'Show me how you would examine and wash such a magnificent organ.'

I had no idea how to do those things in a professional way, of course, so I turned the action into a little drama, remembering how Carlos had let me play with his. And, by turning my wrist, I made it seem to grow erect, from drooping tail to shivering ramrod, fully at attention. That time there was definitely laughter from beyond.

It was a big organ, bigger than Carlos's, and bigger, I think, than most men's, from what comparisons Carlos made. But then if they wanted to test a girl for that work, it would make sense to give her something close to the biggest she might encounter rather than something average or small.

'Well, mam'selle, since you have provoked it into that interesting condition, please proceed. It is begging to be admitted to your mouth, don't you think? How do you cope with that, eh?'

I showed him, for that was something Carlos had taught me well. He loved that sort of play and had shown me all the most sensitive parts of a man, and all the things that give him the greatest delight.

As soon as he saw I knew what to do with my mouth and lips and tongue and teeth – not to mention my tickly little fingers – M Vallodon wasted no more time. 'Let us see how well your other lips can cope,' he commanded. 'Show me how you imagine a man as ardent as that might wish to enter you.'

I straddled the chair with my thighs parted wide and facing the cabinet – and I showed him. Carlos liked to enter me slow-slow-slowly, teasing me with the tip of it, pushing my *vagin* apart and then withdrawing suddenly, making it collapse. I did all those things with that ... dildo? Was that my grandmother's word for it? And I imagined Carlos there in front of me, attached to that engorged organ and thrusting away. Indeed, I was so successful at it that I began to feel my *plaisir* coming on. My labia swelled and went scarlet, and very wet.

'Enough!' The voice was almost in panic. 'Save it!'

'I have no need to save anything, m'sieu. There are dozens more where this one is coming from.'

'Do as you are told, please,' he responded crisply. 'In fact, mam'selle, the test can end here, if you wish. By great good fortune one of my clients has called upon me while you have been in there. For the last ten minutes he has been watching you – and by now the eyes are falling out of his head. He is more than willing to continue the test in person if you are agreeable?'

My heart fell into my boots, though I trust none of my fear showed in my face. If I passed M V's interview, I had hoped for time to go away and prepare myself mentally for a life that, I have to admit, held no great attraction for me at all. But then it suddenly struck me that *this* was perhaps the best way. Time might be more of an enemy to my intentions than a friend. So I laughed, with a lightness I did not feel, and said how splendid, and nothing would give me greater delight – and so forth.

I was still saying it when the ugliest, dirtiest man I had ever seen in my life came sniggering into the room to join me. (I mean gentleman, of course; I've seen scavengers and rag-and-bone men worse, if only just.) I almost fainted at the sight of so much foulness all gathered together in one corrupt, evil-smelling person. I remembered something my grandmother had written – how she coped with those equally dreadful moments in her life. She sought for one bright feature, one element in the man of whom you could say, 'Well, that at least is not too bad.' And then she would concentrate all her attention on that single feature and hope it would obliterate the rest.

Alas, the Baron E. (as he at once introduced himself) lacked any such accommodating virtue. His hair was thin, unkempt, and oily. His skin – what I could see of it, for he was fully clothed as for the opera, cane, hat, silk scarf, and all – could not have seen soap since his nanny last washed it. Nor had the few teeth that remained to him. When he took off one of his gloves he had half a garden under his fingernails. 'Pretty! Pretty!' he grunted as he petted my cheeks with his hairy knuckles.

I summoned up my bravest smile and asked him what would be his pleasure.

He giggled (if a noise so guttural may be called a giggle) and ripped open his flies. To my utter horror, the belly-ruffian that reared towards me from those dank folds – reeking of debauchery – was the very one from which that dildo had been cast! I thanked God I had not eaten that day, or I would now have got my second sight of it all. To think I had been playing with the replica of that! Stuffing it into me – *putting it in my mouth!* I almost passed out as that memory struck me. What if he should tell me *that* was his pleasure now?

And then a most extraordinary thing happened, but for which the entire course of my life might have taken a different turn. I was still pretending to ecstasy for all my worth; starvation is a wonderful mother to deception of every kind. And yet something of my panic must have shown. For my Baron glanced uncertainly toward the cabinet before he went on with our test.

It was so brief I almost missed it, but in that instant I passed from absolute ignorance to absolute understanding. This was no Baron, nor yet no client, either. This was some menial, chosen for his foulness and kept specifically for such tests as this!

Again I am amazed to observe how *the same thing,* when set in a different context can become its very opposite – in the way that my intimation of death with Carlos was, in truth, my climax, and the vile odour became the aroma of fine cheeses. So the 'vile Baron' was really an actor — not unlike myself in that situation. His scrofula might be make-up! The dirt beneath his nails could have been gathered in any flower pot five minutes ago! And to get breath like that — why, I could pick the very cheese to do it (and savour every bite).

But while I was inwardly laughing at these discoveries and the manner in which they would ease me through whatever was to follow, I was assailed by fresh doubts. What, in fact, was the purpose of such tests? Was the would-be courtesan to reveal her finesse and breeding, her ability to discriminate? If I rejected this ape, would that gain me access to his stable? It sounded a fine argument but for one thing: Almost every woman in the civilized world would have drawn the line at such a creature — which would leave M V. either accepting almost every woman who applied, or accepting that tiny band whose sensibilities were so blunted they could go through with it.

(All this crossed my mind in the fraction of a second while the 'Baron' hesitated, waiting for a command or a sign of some kind from his master in that cabinet.) Of course, now that I saw him as an actor, I knew I could go through with our charade — but that was no longer the point at issue.

I could think of no way out of my dilemma; so I decided to go ahead in the hope that something would occur to me before he finished. I threw myself upon my back, my *derrière* on the edge of the bed and my heels on the floor. 'Come on,' I panted. 'I want the real thing inside me now!'

Whatever his master had commanded, he could not have held himself back — seeing such a sweet, young invitation lying so open and helpless before him. With grunts of delight he pushed himself into me and then just went on pushing. God, he almost split me in two! I hastily threw up my legs, placing my heels on his shoulders, one each side of his head. That way I was able to tense my buttocks and keep him from going in so deep. The girth of him I could cope with well enough. Indeed, now I knew him to be a mere actor, I even found a little thrill in it, too. No climax, to be sure – neither great nor small – but a little ripple running up and down me.

He finished off pretty quickly. I believe he got few chances to go so far with the applicants at that house. When he had done, he confirmed my guess as to his status by doing himself up and slinking out like a whipped cur – never a backward glance, nor any of the words and gestures that a real Baron might have made, having taken such delight of a delicate young girl.

I used my douche and wiped myself ostentatiously on those beautiful silk sheets. 'M'sieu,' I said quietly, not deigning to look up. 'Are you still there?'

There was no reply.

I went on: 'I wish to tell you I do not care a fig what your opinion of me may be. I no longer have the slightest intention of working for you.'

'That is a pity, mam'selle,' he replied. 'But naturally, the choice is yours.'

'I do not expect to be paid for the exhibition I made of myself to you …' I left the rest of the thought delicately upon the air and continued with my dressing.

He did not take it up directly. 'I may tell you,' he said, 'I see several young ladies every week. Of course, many more than that apply but Madame Laroche – the maid who let you in – she winnows them down so that I see only the very best …'

'How?' I blurted out.

He laughed. 'You see! Our trade is of *some* interest to you after all.'

'I'm curious,' I admitted.

26

'She describes old Shadraque, my gardener – the "Baron" whom you have now made the happiest man in Paris. She describes him and says he will be their test ...'

'She refused to tell me a thing.'

'Of course! She has an infallible eye for true quality. As I say, she lets through only the very cream. And, as I was *about* to say, before your many interruptions, though I interview perhaps half a dozen hopeful young ladies a week ...'

'Do they all meet Baron Shadraque?'

'Mon Dieu, mam'selle! May I finish my sentence? Let's have a pact. I will tell you what I want to tell you, *then* I will answer any reasonable question, *hein?*'

I dipped my head in apology.

He went on: 'Though I see half a dozen a week, I meet a girl of your quality not once in a whole year. Of course, the choice is absolutely yours – but perhaps now that you know Shadraque was a mere trick and is the very opposite of the sort of gentleman who patronizes my young ladies ... perhaps you will see that your rejection was a little hasty? Pray take your time and think it over. Madame Laroche will give you a thousand francs on your way out.'

I froze in the very act of lacing up my bodice. 'How much?' I could barely get above a whisper.

'A thousand,' he repeated off-handedly. 'It's nothing compared to what you might earn in one night of pleasure. You could be the grandest of *grandes horizontales* ...'

I burst out laughing. 'You must indeed think me very simple, m'sieu. This time last week I was still a virgin. I know *nothing* of the Arts of Venus. Not by any stretch of the imagination could I be worth ...'

'Oh, of course, you have an infinite amount yet to learn. Did you suppose I meant you to start at the very top of the profession? Ah! To be so young again!'

27

I saw the trick then – hang a bucketful of stars before a young girl's eyes, bedazzle her with promises of untold riches 'once she has learned her trade,' and then put her flat on her back for all the traffic she can stand! *Merci m'sieu!*

Of course, I told him I would, indeed, give the matter more thought. Then I asked him what Madame Laroche did with the girls she frightened away.

'She sums them up very skillfully. Then she recommends a particular house where the girl may apply for work more suited to her talent and appearance. All she needs say there is "Madame Laroche sent me …" and they admit her at once.'

'And what becomes of those girls who get as far as *this* chamber but do not pass your scrutiny?'

'Ah! They are still very special young ladies, you know. We generally recommend them to one of those very select houses owned by the Comte de C. The Countess manages them for him now … but, of course, you wouldn't know of them.'

I'm sure my muscles betrayed not the slightest tremor of the astonishment I felt. How close I had come to being despatched, all unknowingly, to the tender care of my own grandmother! 'So many different places!' I mused absently.

'Oh, mademoiselle! Every night in Paris there are sixteen thousand women selling that commodity between their thighs.'

'And how many of them work for you?'

'Eleven at the moment. I have room for twelve. *La crème de la crème!* Do think it over, please.'

Of course, I took a cab back to my hotel in Montmartre. M Vallodon was as good as his word and I now had a thousand francs! *[Over £5,000 in 1980s currency! – FR]* What could it mean? The bait was worth more than the fish. I needed time to think.

I asked myself: If Shadraque had been a genuine client, and for a fee of a thousand francs, would I not have found within myself some way of masking my disgust and doing whatever he might wish, and with every outward show of rapture?

No! I cried.

But then I thought of all the beautiiful things a thousand frances could buy – and that resounding *no* lost some of its echo.

And M Vallodon had promised I should earn even more – and in a single night! And it would be for pleasuring a true gentleman, the very opposite of the loathsome Shadraque. Even if that were the wildest exaggeration – suppose the fee were only five hundred, say – even so, how could I refuse?

The grandest of the *grandes horizontales!* The very idea made my head spin. Yes, I most certainly needed time to think.

But that, it now seemed, was the one commodity I was to be denied, for I had barely transferred all my belongings to the best room in that hotel, and enjoyed a good soak in my bath, before the porter came to me, bearing the card of the Duc de R.

I asked what sort of a man he was. The fellow seemed surprised I did not already know of him. He took me to the window and pointed to an open landau waiting in the street below. The Duc was its sole occupant, attended by his coachman, a page, and two footmen behind, all in the most splendid livery. I doubt such a gorgeous equipage had been seen in that humble street since its paving was laid.

The Duc himself, from what I could see, was in his mid-forties – a lithe, wiry man of about average height. He sat with such nonchalant ease and grace that I already felt a familiar sort of movement, a swelling warmth, somewhere south of my navel. He took off his hat to mop his brow and I saw he had a full head of curly brown hair, slightly frizzy and beautifully cut. As he made to replace his hat he glanced up and saw me standing there, gazing down at him. His eyes were hazel brown, deep-set and very engaging. His nose was thin – aquiline in that aristocratic way of the French ... indeed, his whole face was rather thin. But his mouth was firm and his jaw strong.

And yet it was not a handsome face. Crumpled, full of charm, sympathetic ... it was all of these, but not handsome. It was a face that had known suffering and was now the wiser for it. When at last he smiled and nodded at me, I knew I had no choice but to go down and join him. I stopped only to check I still had my douche in my bag.

I was surprised (and so, I may say, were the footmen) to see him standing beside the carriage, holding open its door for me. 'Have I the honour to address the Honourable Frances Duplessis?' he asked in English – that beautiful English of theirs which we call *broken* – because that is how it so often leaves our hearts. His eyes, close up, were beautiful, too.

I curtsied and replied, in French, that I was, indeed, that suddenly fortunate person.

'I believe I knew your grandmother,' he told me.

I was at once alarmed. No one outside the family is supposed to know of the Countess's connection with us Duplessis. He saw my hesitation and prompted: 'Henrietta, Lady Duplessis – is she not your father's mother?' He seemed alarmed, as if he feared she might be my great-grandmother.

'Yes, of course,' I assured him. 'I see so little of her, you know. For a moment ...' I smiled and didn't bother to complete the thought. What did it matter? All he wanted was to establish that some kind of social intimacy already existed between us, so that he could get to his real point, which was to invite me to dine with him that evening, indeed, that very moment. I accepted without any great show of interest, implying that nothing better had turned up, so why not? That surprised the footmen even more; I began to understand that this duke was not a man to be treated in so cavalier a manner. And yet he seemed to relish it.

As soon as we set off, I inquired if my grandmother, Lady Duplessis, had asked him to seek me out while I was in Paris – thinking that that was the fiction he wished to maintain. But not a bit of it. He spoke to me as if we were completely alone, as if there were not four other pairs of ears straining to catch every word. He said that Captain Lascelles, who had been the arresting officer when they took poor Carlos away, had told him of my predicament and my charms ... so naturally he hoped to be of some assistance to me. He was sure he could offer me a position in his household.

I did not remember giving Carlos my Duplessis name; in fact, I was sure I had used only the 'Plessy'

31

form under which our family prefers to travel, semi-incognito. On the other hand, I had told M Vallodon the truth, thinking, rather foolishly, that my courtesy title of Honourable might stand me in good stead.

I thanked the Duke and told him I was well provided for – at least for the present moment. 'If you consent to become my mistress,' he told me nonchalantly – with those stone gargoyles of servants listening to every word, '*then* you will know what "well provided" actually means.'

'And if I do not?'

'Then we shall still have enjoyed a pleasant evening together, I trust. And Jacques will drive you back to your hotel. The choice is entirely yours – as, naturally, it must be.'

He began to talk of his family … its many branches, their contribution to the glorious history of France, and every now and then he drew a parallel between us – my descent, on the Duplessis side, from a bastard of Charles I, his from a bastard of François I, and so on. He knew all the battles, too. It was fascinating to listen to but I've forgotten most of it. I just sat there beside him, letting that marvellous voice wash over me, talking of so many illustrious events, and I wondered what he was going to look like without his clothes.

When we arrived at his house, I had the explanation of his visit, for he lives almost opposite M Vallodon in the Champs Élysées. True, it is a wide street, and there are two lines of trees in the way, but an ardent man with a good pair of binoculars could take his pick of M Vallodon's applicants. A friendly arrangement ... a name and address ... it could all be done so discreetly. I thought of M Vallodon's assertion that there were sixteen thousand women selling their bodies in Paris that evening. The duke could have had his pick of them – especially *la crème de la crème* from over the way. So why had he gone to all this trouble to select me? What impossible thing was he seeking, which he hoped I might have rather than any other among those sixteen thousand, so experienced and so readily available? It was absurd.

It was also distinctly thrilling. I was glad I had put my silk stockings and those gorgeously revealing drawers back on again after my bath. I could hardly wait to see his eyes, in that moment when I would at last allow him to feast them down there.

He brought me inside, again permitting no one else to open and close the doors for me. I can say now – it is a highly effective gambit. I had thought we would go at once to his bedchamber and see if a bargain between us were possible. But no, he proceeded to show me the entire house! He took me through one exquisite room after another, pausing only long enough in each to pick out one or two of its splendours – a table that had been Louis XVII's, a bas-relief above a door, by Archer, a gift of the Third Duke of Bedford, and so on.

I wondered why he was taking all this trouble over a transaction that must, in his sort of life, be almost as common as eating. Not that I was bored – quite the reverse. Indeed, by then I believe I was even

more in love with that beautiful house than with its master. And then it suddenly dawned upon me why he was behaving like this. It was for the same reason I might have given for such a delay: He was denying himself a pleasure in order to intensify it.

I was overjoyed. My grandmother's letters had led me to believe men were always so ardent and impetuous. I did not think there was any man on earth capable of that finesse. I stared at him with redoubled admiration and now could hardly contain myself to be at our clicket together. A man whose sensibilities were so close to my own – a man, moreover, with vastly greater experience than me – must surely be able to raise me to the seventh heaven with him. Again and again I caught him looking at me – no doubt savouring the thought of undressing me, caressing me, insinuating his fingers between my chastely clenched thighs … placing me in this position or that, and doubling our joys.

At last the tour had brought us to his bedchamber. He announced the fact coolly and, instead of pointing out some especially noteworthy feature, said, 'Perhaps you would now like to eat a little, mam'selle?' When he addressed me in French, which was not often, he called me 'vous.' That made me feel particularly worthy and equal to him.

There was no archness in his question, no simpering sugggestion that 'of course, we both knew what I would truly like to do.' He tried to sound as nonchalant as he had been on

the rest of our tour, but the postponement had had the same effect on him as it had on me. By now we were each trembling with our desire for the other. I just shook my head, no longer capable of speech.

We drifted to the vast bed, though the bedspread – of shot silk, peach on gold – spilled over it and onto an elegant chaise longue, sprinkled with silk and velvet cushions in black, crimson, and peach. I expected him to begin with me on the chaise longue and move onto the bed later; that is what Carlos would have done. But no, he lifted me up in those strong, lithe arms and laid me reverently down on the bed, as far in as he could reach.

'Shall I draw the curtains?' he asked.

I shook my head and went on staring at him, still unwilling to trust my voice.

Our bodies were tired of finesse. We undressed each other, not hastily, but without the languor and the endless tiny postponements I would ordinarily have wished for. We caressed and kissed each new part of our bodies as our clothes fell away, but they were just kisses of welcome, a first step into familiarity; nothing we might have done could possibly have raised our desire any further, and we both realized it, so we wasted little time on those usual preliminaries. And at last we knelt naked before each other. He was unadorned; my stockings and drawers kept alive for us the illusion that the final barrier to

my surrender had yet to be breached. He needed no decoration. I had seen only one other naked man in my life but even so I knew I was hardly likely to see another as fine as the duke. His organ was the most incredibly beautiful thing to me, throbbing away in front of him, making those casual dips and bobs a fencing master makes with his rapier between assaults. It was the first I had seen with an entire foreskin – though it was pushed half back because the knob had grown so huge. I went down on my haunches like a worshipper – and, yes, indeed, I *did* worship that marvellous organ. I circled it with my fingers, as gently as I could, and slowly drew the rest of the foreskin back. It was so shiny and deep-red and urgent-looking – and so hot on my tongue. While I lingered on the sensitive under-parts with my lips and teeth I cupped his tenderest flesh in the cage of my other hand and stroked him with feather-light fingers.

He just knelt there, moaning quietly, eyes closed, face raised to the heavens, mouth open and gasping. When we fell back onto the bed I thought he would go into me at once; but he dived between my thighs and put his gaping mouth to my rosebud of pleasure. That tongue was like five fingers. He could make it go flat and hard, flat and soft, or curled; he could turn it over on its back, both ways, or make a tube of it whose edges would catch up my flesh and send paroxysms of joy reverberating through me; he could curl the tip of it over and grip me until I wanted to beg him to stop.

At one point he raised his head and said, 'You have the sweetest little *cutte* I ever saw. And the taste of you is like nectar.' He called me 'vous,' which was as thrilling to me as before.

At last, when he saw what helpless abandonment his love-play had brought me to, he moved up until our two heads were side by side. I looked down and caught the briefest glimpse of that gorgeous magic wand again; I wanted to go down there and feast on it once more –

but the moment I felt it press against my labia, that desire was replaced by one even more urgent: all I now yearned for was to feel that superb organ moving deep, deep within me.

Oh, he knew how to enlarge all my pleasures – for it was exactly the same way with him. He pushed his *pacquet d'amour* so slowly into me that I felt every little ridge and fold of flesh – his and mine – rubbing and riding together as they passed. And it filled me even better than Carlos's had done, for the knob was bigger and the root of it, against his pelvic bone, smaller. When I closed around him and gripped him, I felt more filled, more stretched, and yet more comfortable with it than I ever had with my poor dear C, whom I had thought so wonderful.

And the rhythms he knew! He, or those superb instincts of his – for I think he was as heedless of mere technique by now as me – waited for each of my thrills and somehow 'got under' it, lifting me up to heights I had never suspected were there. And it wasn't just the friction that did it – nothing mechanical like that. At one point the early-evening sun reflected off a dome on the roof of a fine house somewhere over the road; it shone directly in upon us, a shaft of fire without heat. It showed the beauty of him to perfection – his head, which was so noble and endearing, and the fine muscles of his chest and shoulders, gleaming with our sweat and rippling like liquid gold.

Time and again I thought I could reach no greater climax and, when the shuddering was over, I settled to encourage him in his. But he was tireless. He would just move me into a new position and start all over again. I don't suppose any of my climaxes was really any greater than the rest; but when they are all so magnificent, each one, as its moment comes, feels like the greatest since the beginning of the world. We rolled down onto the chaise longue, where he placed my lower ribs against the sloping back and my head, resting on my arms, on the bed, leaving my breasts hanging in the free space between. Then he went in from behind; with one hand he worked on both my nipples while the other went down to my clitoris. That one almost killed me, I swear.

Another time he laid me on my back with my *derrière* on the edge of the bed; then he knelt between my thighs on one of the velvet pillows and moved himself in and out as fast as he could, never going in very far. I was just beginning to wonder if he would ever have his own thrill when yet another climax racked me – taking me completely unawares.

When I came round from that I found we were back on the bed and I was on top, straddling him while he just lay there gasping and exhausted. I started a circular movement of my hips, moving up and down at the same time, which forced his knob hard against each wall of my civet in turn. I thought that would surely make him climax, but instead – bang! There I was again, collapsed on him in a pool of sweat and fighting to get my heartbeat back where it belonged.

And then he returned to our first position of all, with him on top of me and pressing me deep into the mattress; but this time I had a little pillow beneath me, so that my rosebud was in constant contact with the base of his *joujou*; and there he let me ride one small orgasmic wave after another – nothing earth-shattering like before, just a long, gentle, downward ride, now moving into a climax, now coming out again, almost like being on a swing and passing regularly back and forth between full sunlight and deep shade.

Suddenly, just when I was sure he'd hold himself back for another session later that night, he went as rigid as iron and moaned, 'Oh ... oh ... oh!' into the furnace of my ear. I could feel it coming into me, each separate squirt. And his pelvis thrust deep with each one; and my hands clutched his hard, tight little buttocks and tried to pull him even deeper.

When it was over he fell away from me, lay exhausted on his back, gasped once or twice, and then turned to me once more. And he cradled me in his arms and we fell asleep, not waking until it was dark and the cool of the evening nudged us back into the world.

We rose, dressed, and ate a light supper (and in that Parisian heat no other sort of meal was possible). Then we went out for a walk along the banks of the Seine, under the stars. At the Pont Marly we stopped and watched the moon-silvered ripples casting nets over the water, the stonework, and the overhanging trees.

'You are only the second man I have lain with,' I told him.

'I cannot think of it in those terms,' he replied. 'To me, every woman is unique. You are the first.'

'It's easy to say that after so many. In fact, you probably have to say it to ease your conscience.'

He laughed. 'Why should I need to ease my conscience?'

'Because you did not find whatever you were seeking with them? Else why go on?'

He was silent after that.

'Am I right, monsieur?' I asked. 'Have there been so many "first times"?'

He shrugged – I heard the gesture in his voice without turning to look at him. 'Perhaps too many.'

'And you must be looking for something?'

Again he did not answer.

'Did you find any of it – whatever you're seeking – did you find it with me?'

Reluctantly he spoke: 'If I tell you the truth, you'll remember my admission that I've known too many women, and you'll say to yourself, "Well, naturally, he always tells them that." *Alors!*'

'You think I'm too young to judge you properly?'

He turned to me then and took me in his arms, shivering. He held me such a long time, as if he dared not speak. At last he whispered, 'I think I have found in you, mam'selle, what I have been seeking all these years. And that is truly something I have never said to any other woman.'

He turned me away from him then, but only so that he could embrace me from the side, and a little behind me, with our cheeks pressed gently together. 'It is not only what we did in my chamber this evening ... indeed, that hardly comes into it. I hope I can explain it. I hope you will understand. What I have been seeking all these years is a woman who is ... *beyond* me in every possible way.'

'But, Monsieur le Duc!' I protested.

'No, no – listen! You are *not* that woman – or you are not that woman *yet*. But I believe the only thing that prevents you from becoming her is your lack of experience. What we *did* together – the mechanical act of my moving myself in and out of you and procuring pleasure by it – that could be achieved with any one of a thousand women ...'

'Sixteen thousand,' I interrupted. 'If what M Vallodon told me is correct.' I mentioned that old gentleman's name because I wanted to see how my darling Duke reacted to it.

He chuckled. 'Ah! Monsieur Vallodon! I suppose you saw through my little white lie at once.'

'I did not tell Carlos my full name – only that I'm called Plessy. But it was kind of you – that's what I saw at once. You did not wish me to realize you knew I had visited that man for *that* purpose. You are truly kind.'

'You see? That is precisely what I mean about you. You ... go beyond most other people. It's the only way I can put it. In some of the things you say you are as naïve as any young peasant girl up from the provinces, and yet in your soul you are as cunning as old Eve herself. You perceive things in people, instantly, without thought ... you perceive things that others spend a lifetime training themselves to spot. Vallodon and that old maid of his, Madame Laroche – they have an infallible nose for the characters of young girls. They have to, of course, or they'd soon be out of business. And they told me that of the thousands they have seen over the years, you stood out at once.'

I had, and, indeed, still have, no idea what he was talking about; but it was typical of his infinite charm to go on in such an extravagant way.

He continued: 'Vallodon says you "failed" his test in the most spectacular fashion – and then calmly sat down, got dressed, and told him you would – after such an encounter – never consider working for him, no matter what he offered. By saying that – as I'm sure you knew very well – you were rewriting your name at the very top of his list. Even if he had had twelve fillies, he'd have kicked one out to make room for you.'

I was bewildered by now. His words no longer sounded like the babble of charming flattery. I could almost believe he actually meant it. 'I can't see much art in that,' I said. 'I could tell from the way that awful creature Shadraque kept glancing toward his master that he was no real client – just part of the test. The question was, did I pass it by rejecting him or by accepting him?'

'An impossible dilemma, mam'selle. And yet, on the spur of the moment, you found a way to make it come right, either way. And not just right, but *superbly* right. That's what I mean: You immediately go beyond the surface of the situation. You understand the people, the drama, and you place yourself at once in the heart of it.'

I laughed. 'I didn't get into the heart of poor Carlos. He really deceived me.'

'Yes?' His tone was disbelieving. 'I think you saw at once he was no good but, in the same twinkling of your bright, come-to-bed eyes, you also saw how that left you free – free to get from him whatever you wanted for that week. Are you heartbroken at what has become of him?'

'No.' I had to admit it.

'*Voilà!* I cannot think of any other girl your age who would not have fallen madly in love with such a man – and be desolated by his arrest.'

I sighed. 'I must put all this down in my diary. I don't think I can begin to understand my thoughts, you know, until I see them written down.'

And then, when we came back to his house – although I could see he was bursting (almost literally) with desire for me, and I was far from indifferent to him – he nonetheless insisted I sit here and write it all down, as I am doing at this moment. What a wonderful man!

Do I love him? He fills my world and my thoughts; that is all I can say. I feel certain that a strange destiny has brought us together; but will it be enough to keep us there? For me, I think so, and yet something in his eyes, those knowing, come-to-bed

eyes of his, says that in my case it will not. I wrote
that because he is now standing behind me, reading
this over my shoulder. I don't mind. I don't want to
conceal a single thought from him. And my present
thought, at this exact moment in my life – looking
under my arm at the distressed state of his nightshirt
– is that his *fusil* is desperate to renew its introduction to my *belle chose* – my beautiful, soft,
squirming, throbbing, hot, wet, dark, secret, how do
you spell oleaginous and is that the right word

[*Here a different hand has written:*]
Yes, indeed, mademoiselle, that Favour is craved so
very, very deeply by my hot, hard, urgent, demanding,
imperious, scarlet-knobbed

[*After a blot, Fanny continues:*]
All the ink in this well, even were it bottomless,
could not describe the sweet foreboding with which
my dearest *petit trou* awaits her second encounter
with

[*And the other hand concludes with:*]
But for me it will be the first time again!

The heat has broken at last and we can resume our
normal lives again. But what is a *normal* life any
more? Is it normal to spend day and night thinking
about sexual pleasure? I have not read a book, been
to the theatre, entertained anyone, looked at the
papers ... well, we have been out for drives in our
carriage and I have bought more dresses than Paris
could sell. They had to send to London, Rome,
Vienna, to satisfy my demands. (Not quite, but it
nearly came to that.) And the enticing lingerie the
Duke has bought for my adornment! If I cannot see
myself through his eyes now, then I am blind indeed.

In fact – and jesting apart now – that is what I
suddenly need to communicate with myself through
this strange medium of my diary. Dear Diary – tell
me what to think!

Three weeks ago if I had tried to guess how I
should spend this intervening period – remembering
I had just met the most wonderful lover, as rich as
the Bank of France (richer, he says), whose nerves
seem to unite with my own so that the delight of

either is at once the delight of both – remembering all that, what might I have guessed? That we should spend whole days in bed together? That we should eat only to revive our exhausted powers? And bathe only to remove the glue of our uttermost pleasuring? And that I should become one of Paris's foremost savants in the subject of ... photography?

Hein?

Quoi?

Photography?

Yes! With the sun and heat as our allies, we have spent the last three weeks naked together, pleasuring ourselves in every possible attitude and capturing the moments in grains of silver bromide on sheets of glass. And I can now prepare those sheets of glass, mask them in their holders, slip them into the camera, judge the exposure, touch the little clockwork mechanism that delays the removal of the lens covers (all our pictures are for viewing in the stereoscope) until the Duke and I are in position, and then hold still for as long as is needed. Then I can change the plates and go again, and again, and again ... And then I can develop them and fix them. Fix! Is that not a beauteous word? All our most magic moments captured and *fixed* into history's archive. (Actually, posing for these photographs was, for both of us, the most maddeningly splendid postponement of pleasure we could possibly have devised. After each session beneath those peeping-tom lenses we were both ready to devour each other, out of their sight, down in our bed. But that is by the way.)

To use up the last few plates of each session the Duke liked me to photograph his *flageolet*, still rock-hard, peering up at my twin lenses as if wondering was there a new way into me via them. And then we would change places and he would take several of me offering myself to their twin, poking snouts; I felt like a drunken maid seeing double. His favourite poses were from behind, with me kneeling forward and poking my *derrière* at the lens. In the first one I have my hand thrust up between my thighs with the fingers clamping my labia tight together; in the second one those same fingers are spreading them as wide as they'll stretch. He can put on the stereo glasses and stare at those two for hours. And I could look at them coolly and tell any professional photographer in Paris what *bellows extension factor* the Duke had to use to get that perfect *exposure* of me.

But my serious point is that, after some hours of looking at myself as a third person, me-as-voyeuse watching me-as-amante, I have somehow acquired a masculine perception of the sexual act itself. I don't mean this new perception has replaced my own, innate view of it as a woman. It is *supplémentaire* – an extra understanding grafted on to my own, available to me at will. When the Duke and I are pleasuring each other, even at the height of our passion, some part of me can become him and I can now imagine myself *as him enjoying me!* And when it happens, it does not, as I say, efface my own pleasure *as me enjoying him,* but rather it intensifies it even more.

No. That is hopelessly confused. Writing things down does not always help. Still. It is there now. I can reread it ... add notes. Someday I will understand. Meanwhile ... enjoy.

It is true – I, too, have lost count of the number of times the Duke and I have now lain together. And each time *is* like a first time. And yet, as autumn draws on in the world outside, I feel a kind of autumnal mellowing of our love. He is as ardent as ever and yet he is worrying about me in some way. Does he fear I will leave him? Or is he afraid to put his heart utterly in my hands in case I, with all my youth and inexperience, may break it? Can I blame him? But how can I reassure him?

Today (October 4th – I must get in the habit of dating these jottings. Already I could not be sure to give the right dates to the above), he said to me that he could never give me all the experiences I need. I told him I had already had a thousand times more experiences with him than any girl my age could possibly expect (though, of course, we would all *desire* it). (Actually, I wonder if that is true? I have known some girls who, I'm sure, never feel the slightest desire. I think I was given the portions intended for a hundred of them, for my appetite only grows on what feeds it.) He replied that I would not always be 'a young girl my age' – and that was his whole point. Is this a polite way of preparing me to make way for my successor in his bed?

Monday, October 21st, 1850.
What a naïve thought that was! He was, of course, preparing me for something much more complicated than that – as I might have guessed if I had only one tenth as much perception as he credits me with.

Last Monday night as we lay in bed talking (for once) about our pleasuring instead of doing it, he suddenly said, 'Don't you think you owe M Vallodon a favour?'

'Do I?' I asked, very surprised to hear it.

'But for him you might now be a mere courtesan, *La plus grande des grandes horizontales*. Nothing more than that.'

47

'Whereas?' I teased.

'Whereas you have metamorphosed into the Goddess of Love herself. Don't you think Venus owes poor mortal Vallodon a little favour?'

'Poor mortal?' I echoed in disbelief. 'Him?'

He did not respond to my challenge but gathered his thoughts awhile in silence. 'D'you know why he does what he does?' he asked at length.

'For money?' I guessed.

'Not at all. He only takes ten centimes in the franc from his fillies. That still leaves him a rich man, of course, but he could be five times richer. Most men in his trade – one hesitates to put them into the same category, for they are pimps and he is not – but most such men take at least fifty in the franc. Some, I know, take every last centime.'

'Why do the women permit it?' I asked indignantly.

'Ah!' he said with infinite sadness, stroking my hair as if I were a cat. 'So, if it is not for money – why does he do it?'

'Mme Laroche told me he loves all women.'

'Hah! He wishes he could! Yes – that is what drives him. He wishes he could love all women. He thinks of it day and night. It obsesses him. He remembers the time when he could enjoy four women a day with the greatest ease, every day, year after year. And it broke him in the end ...'

'We've enjoyed each other a lot more than four times a day, my dear. And ...'

'Yes, I've been meaning to talk to you about that! I am not as young as I used to be – and certainly not as young as you. But let's stick to poor Vallodon for the moment. D'you know how he gets his sexual thrills nowadays?'

I suddenly saw it. 'By conducting his tests! He sits there behind that china cabinet and watches. He's

48

turned into nothing but a voyeur. The *crème de la crème* – his courtesans and their "highly paid positions" – that's just so much bait to bring the young girls flocking to join them. The artful old thing! I believe he owes *me* a favour now.'

The Duke said nothing.

'Am I not right?' I pressed.

'I think you should see it for yourself,' he replied. 'You would learn ... so much.'

I was now in a quandary. 'Do you command it?' I asked.

'I will never command you anything. You know that. But I advise it. If you wish to unravel the nature of your own sexual desire, you must – in the end – understand the desires of others. As many others as you can manage – and I think your capacity in that direction is high.'

'Will I have to pleasure Vallodon himself?'

'Indirectly.'

'By lying with someone else?'

He laughed in surprise. 'How do you do it? You read my mind. You are there already.'

'Not Shadraque again!'

'No – your lover will be as handsome and lively a young man as you could ever wish to open your thighs for. A cavalry officer – a genuine cavalry officer this time.'

'And you would not mind?' I asked, already feeling a little excited at the prospect.

'I told you. It goes far beyond "minding" and "not minding." This is to increase your enlightenment.'

Next evening, before I went over to Vallodon's, he said, 'This is the first of many adventures I hope you will undertake. This one, I can almost guarantee, will be nothing but pleasant. The others? Maybe. But each of them will show you something you could have learned in no other way. And remember – while I live, I am always here. I am yours now, my darling Fanny, until I die.'

I kissed him tenderly and there were tears welling up in my eyes as we parted. And yet – I must be honest or there is no point in keeping this record – if he had now begged me not to go and promised me a whole night of pleasuring with him, I would nonetheless have gone. I was on fire with a new desire. For the cavalry officer? A little. But mostly for the new experience.

Mme Laroche fawned on me in a most embarrassing way. The entire household seemed in a state of nerves, as if *my* visit were something utterly out of the ordinary. And yet, if what the Duke had said was true, then some young girl called at this house every Tuesday, Thursday, and Saturday, to do exactly what I was about to do. A different one each time, I mean.

I thought at first Madame was leading me to the octagonal room and my heart sank; but she smiled at me and went on by, knowing what dire forebodings had crossed my mind. She paused at a door a little farther down the passage and, putting her finger to her lips, motioned me to approach it as quietly as I could.

There was a little spyhole at a convenient height, formed by the removal of a knot in the grain of one of the panels. Through it I saw an exceedingly dashing young man in full cavalry officer's uniform, broad-shouldered, dark-haired and with intense, deep-set eyes. He was striding up and down, one hand gloved, the other bare, pulling nervously at the empty fingers. My cranny already grew warm and melting at the mere sight of him.

Lying on a vast bed nearby was an elderly gentle-man, quite naked. This, I knew, was Vallodon, for the whole arrangement had been explained to me. Sitting at his side, as I also expected, was a handsome young boy. He, too, was naked, and his knob was already stiff and red – perfect, I thought, for a lad of his age. He sat there, ignoring it entirely, watching my officer and gently, almost abstractedly, massaging Vallodon's spine, up and down, with the tips of the fingers of his left hand.

I had been told to ignore Vallodon completely and behave as if the officer and I were alone for our assignation, so I now took my only chance to examine the old boy. He looked like the death mask of Voltaire, but with the sight restored to his eyes, and a perky, jaunty look they had, too. I took an instant liking to him, to his feeble shoulders, his lank hair, his pigeon chest, his shrivelled buttocks – and even to the limp *goupillon*, which I glimpsed from time to time. There was something about him – I had even detected it in his disembodied voice – that made me want to befriend him.

I withdrew my eye and nodded my thanks to Madame; then, taking a deep breath, I put my trembling hand to the doorknob. My officer spun around at my entry. His eyes took me in at a single glance, and I'll never forget the look of rapture that suddenly spread over his face. What had he feared? He knew Vallodon chose only pretty girls for these occasions. So what did he see in me that was such an overwhelming joy to him? Whatever it was, that pleasure in his face made me his for the night.

He crossed the room to me at once and took my hand up to his lips. He introduced himself to me as Dion de B. and added that friends called him Dino; he, too, called me 'vous,' which was always one key to my consent. I told him I was called Phillide – and then instantly regretted lying. But it was too late.

He led me across to the bed and, falling to his knees, implored me to grant him the favour of permitting a kiss, one single kiss ... he had pined for me so long, so long!

Because it was a play that we made up as we went along, I found the whole charade absurdly easy. I invented his parents and asked him the most detailed questions. Not intimate, but things like had his father recovered from his fall near the beehives last week. And he, quick as a flash, took it up, asking me if my mother had enjoyed the novel his aunt had sent her ... and so on.

And all this while we were removing each other's clothing, slowly, lovingly, lingeringly – and kissing and caressing whatever lay beneath. I now had on some of my most enticing lingerie – the sight of which almost threw him off the horse of his invention. Just the *weight* of his ardour, of his dark gaze, on the tops of my breasts, and boring like delicate little needles into the topmost millimetre of my nipples, which was all that was visible, made me breathless. And when at last I permitted him to take off my final petticoat and explore with his eyes and fingers and lips my delectable labiate lady, my shrouded clitoris, my silently screaming cunnie –

well, I thought he would spend himself at once, so ardent had his glances grown. And what a pretty pickle that would have been.

But the body's basic instinct is miserly after all, and he hoarded his discharge for its proper investment. I lay back with a sigh of genuine ecstasy and started to caress my own breasts – to give me another focus and prevent myself from cracking his head like a nut between my thighs. My first *plaisir* was small and sweet, and I knew at once they would all be like that. I was glad, in fact – for I didn't want to lose control in front of Vallodon. My time would come later.

And so we went at it, Dino and I – placing ourselves in every convenient position we could devise in that great, soft bed. And all the while Vallodon crouched nearby, down on on his knees and elbows, watching intently. *Remembering,* as the Duke had expressed it. And the young lad lay on his back beyond his master and, reaching in under him, pulled at the old man's flaccid *goupillon* with long, gentle strokes, lubricating it with juice borrowed, as it were, from Dino and me. Vallodon, for his part, grabbed the lad's peg as if he would lose his way without it.

In the corner of our eyes both Dino and I were watching this other drama, even as we were acting out our own. Instinctively we were both taking our time from its rhythm, breathing harder as Vallodon's eyes grew wilder. I did not know a man could spend out of a limp organ, but – if it is a technique – Vallodon had perfected it; I noticed that his *goupillon* went stiff for a fraction of a second just before each squirt. The lad had perfected his technique, too. Of course, boys that age can spend at the drop of a hat, or so the Duke had explained. He said he, at that age, had once found the barking of a dog on a warm summer evening so incredibly erotic it had made him spend into his trousers before he could stop himself.

So there was Vallodon, spending limply into a towel he had spread beneath him; and there was the lad, pumping himself away into his master's hand, whimpering with each pulse. And there was Dino, going mad on me – and I knew it was all fake because I could feel how he had shrivelled almost to nothing inside me. I didn't let the old firm down, though.

When Dino and I had recovered from what had not, after all, happened between us, we found we were alone – though not for long. Madame Laroche came bustling in with a jug of warm water, humming a little tune to herself. 'You were the best for a long time,' she told us happily, setting the water down in the wash-stand basin. 'Now rest assured you are entirely alone until you ring in the morning. No one will be watching you.' And to underline the point she pulled a little green curtain over the knothole on our side of the door.

When we had washed and were back in bed, Dino said to me, 'Oh Mademoiselle Phillide, what must you think of me?'

'Dino,' I murmured. 'Call me just Fanny, for that is my real name. I was too shy to give it before those other two – just as you were too shy to give me your true self while they were here.' I laid my hand lightly on his thigh and began to caress him lingeringly with my fingernails. The Duke had shown me a nerve on the inside of a man's thigh that will make his testicles leap with pleasure – and that will almost always procure an erection if the potency is there for it.

It was.

Dino watched in incredulous delight.

'You must understand,' I told him. 'I have lain with only two other men in my life, so I do not judge you from any great pinnacle of experience.'

'Only two?' he asked, puzzled. 'But are you not one of Vallodon's courtesans?'

I shook my head. 'I am the mistress of the Duc de R. He asked me to oblige Vallodon like this. I said I would if I could see the young man first – and only then if he excited me.' I pointed to the green curtain. 'That now covers the spyhole I used.'

'Oh but – Mademoiselle Fanny. The mistress of ... but now you must think even worse of me – for I simply assumed I now had the right to commandeer your body for the night. Will you ever forgive me? What can I say?'

I smiled up at him. 'There is a large, rather urgent-looking monsieur down here who is speaking most eloquently for you, Dino my dear. And if I'm to be allowed any say in the matter, then ...'

And I sucked the whole of him into my mouth and swallowed the knob of him down into my gullet, where I swallowed and swallowed ... three, four, five times – at which he gave a little moan and spent himself copiously.

I don't know which of us begged the other for mercy first, but it was well past midnight by then, and our revels had started at eight.

I have torn out the last two pages, which gave a detailed description of what we did. This diary is not to deteriorate into a simple catalogue of my sexual *gymnastique*. It is about what those exercises teach me – about myself, my own sexuality, if there is such a word, and about sex in general.

So what did my wonderful night with Dino teach me? Not teach. Teaching brings something new. Reveal is the word.

It revealed something very ancient within me: I am closer to my grandmother in my sensual nature than I have liked to imagine. By no stretch of the imagination could I be said to love Dino. He stirred much within me, but not a particle of my romantic nature. Instead he drew aside a veil on my soul and showed, lurking there, an almost boundless well of sensuality. I think now that I could spend a night with almost any man provided he were *sympatique,* was moderately well endowed (physically, I mean), and absolutely *adored* me!

How I love the mute, sexual adoration of men; to feel their hooded eyes, heavy with the weight of lust, upon me; to know that the mere sight and fragrance of me has stirred them into a turmoil, so that they shiver, lose their focus, forget their words – and all because they have suddenly become obsessed with the notion of getting their lovely, hot, hard joysticks into me. Me! It is a miracle I can still hardly believe – that just by being, I can do all that to them.

On Thursday night Vallodon has asked me to go back and meet another young officer from the same regiment. Already I can hardly wait for this encounter. The Duke sees me slipping from him into this great sea of sensual advanture. Well, he pushed me into it first. I love him still. I think I shall never truly love another. But now I am into its warmth I must swim there until I tire.

I liked the look of the second young officer even more than Dino. He was a short, powerful little bull-terrier of a man with a clipped moustache, fiercely waxed, and a gold monocle. He lay sprawled at his ease in a chair, puffing at a cheroot and blowing smoke rings into the air; his favourite trick was to blow one big lazy ring and then inject a swifter, smaller ring through it – something which, in that context, was already powerfully erotic.

Here's a new sort of man for me altogether, I thought. *Strong and masterful. Knows what he wants. He might even be a bit rough with me.* I began to tremble with more than the usual sort of anticipation. My desire was coloured with fear as I put my hand to the door and went in.

He sprang to attention and bowed stiffly from the waist. 'De la Tour, mam'selle,' he barked.

'Mlle Plessis, monsieur,' I said, eyeing him nervously. 'Victorine Plessis.'

There was no finesse about him – no attempt to make a little playlet of it for Vallodon's benefit. But then he needed no such prop. He was all energy – raw, hungry, sexual energy. He undid my blouse and stared at my breasts ... and the force of his pleasure, the power of his longing, was like a hot blast upon me. I felt my will beginning to shrivel, my soul, my self – everything that was me and that could stand apart from my sexual being; all of it withered under the heat of his lust and primal fire. I, too, was reduced to the overheated core of my own sexuality; I was a shriek of longing, a cry for him to come and unite with me and make us one.

For him, Vallodon truly did not exist – and soon he made it so for me, too. Was he rough with me? His behaviour passed into a realm that lay beyond such judgements. Certainly I remember his great, demanding hands clasping me from behind, almost crushing my hips with their strength as he hauled me onto him. I remember him ramming hard into me, again and again, grunting like a god and telling me how superb I was. My ears had climaxes. The nape of my neck had climaxes. I climaxed in the small of my back. My knees expired with the thrill of it all ... until at last I lay there, shattered and exhausted at what we had done.

I think I saw Vallodon and the lad take their silent leave. When I began to recover myself I found de la Tour sitting in the chair again, stark naked, leaning against his carefully folded tunic, and borrowing, as it were, the monocle that was attached to it, to enable him to scan a gossip magazine. I was reminded of those pugilists who look so fierce and dedicated while they are fighting – until the referee calls the end of the round; and then they go off nonchalantly to their seconds and gossip like any group of street-corner politicians. De la Tour's sexual ferocity suddenly acquired that sort of quality.

'*Tiens!*' he said amiably. 'I did well, I see. And now, mam'selle, I claim my reward.'

I would love to be able to record at this point that I shouted up and down the banks in my fury ... screamed at him ... asked him who the devil he thought he was – who the devil he thought *I* was ... got dressed ... stormed out in a huff. The oddest thing of all is that that is precisely what I did do! And yet I so nearly did not. For what was a split second to him, and to me an eternity, I teetered on the brink of falling beneath his spell – of letting that incredible reservoir of sexual skill and passion flood over me all night (I'm sure he was an all-night man). And I still cannot say why the decision went the other way; for certainly all the voices I could hear in my mind's ear were singing the other siren song, urging me to yield.

And yet I did storm out, clutching my clothes to me and hobbling into my court shoes as I went. He followed me, naked as he was, but I closed the door of the octagonal room in his face and turned the thumb bolt firmly against him. While he stood out there in the light, asking me what sort of game I thought I was playing, I, there in the pitch dark, put on my clothes at my leisure and said nothing. When I was ready, I tested my nerves and was surprised to find them icy calm. I opened the door and stared him coolly up and down.

He was completely taken aback to find me dressed again. 'Well?' he asked, but he did not speak half as imperiously as he wished to, I'm sure.

'You, monsieur, have done the one unpardonable thing. You have assumed my availability.'

He laughed. 'What sort of whore are you, then?'

I swept past him. 'I am no sort of whore at all. Ask Vallodon. Even he couldn't get me.'

All the way down that passage my hot little civet was begging me to turn round, apologize, go back, and crave another dose of that incredible medicine. Yet, curiously enough, I felt able to assure her that (I know not how) she and I had not (and have not) felt the last of M de la Tour.

The Duke, who was glad enough to *stand in* and console me, was both amused and amazed at my story; de la Tour, he says, is one of the richest young men in France.

'As rich as you?' I asked.

'Hardly!' And he smiled and laid me gently but firmly on my back and proved it.

You would think that, what with all the pleasuring that has gone on between men and women since the beginning of time, we would by now have a hundred different words to describe its many qualities. We have them for the gratification of our other senses. Think of all the words there are to describe the qualities of the foods we eat or the sounds we hear. But with sex we do not even have the equivalent of salty, or sweet, or acidic – the three most basic tastes of all in food.

How sad! The sexual thrill I enjoyed with de la Tour was like nothing else I had ever known. What I later enjoyed with the Duke was like many another sweet encounter between our bodies. Was the one better than the other? Not a bit. I know which I should chose as my staple diet (to take the analogy from food); but I would be sad, indeed, if I thought that other dish would never come my way again.

This morning at breakfast (Tuesday, 1st November, by the way) he passed me a letter without comment. I had to look at it several times before I could believe my eyes. It was from my grandmother! She made inquiries after receiving my letter and, through the sexual catacombs of this fair city, got to learn of my whereabouts and would call to congratulate me that very afternoon – if the Duke would permit her to enter after their last little contretemps!

'What happened?' I asked him.

'Why didn't you let me know?' he asked, hurt at what he took to be my secretiveness.

'It was my grandmother's wish, not mine. I would not feel slighted to learn you'd kept some family secrets from me – which, indeed, I'm sure you have.'

He dipped his head in reluctant concession.

'Will you bar the door to her?'

He smiled again and said no.

'What happened between you?'

'She enticed a lover of mine into working for her. It hardly matters now.'

'Did the girl go of her own free will?'

He nodded.

'And did she enjoy the new life?'

'Yes. I knew even less about women then than now.'

'What in particular?'

'That some women are born for that sort of life. Not for its sexual possibilities, you understand. They need the comradeship, that strange mixture of adventure and routine – the endlessly repetitive act, the numbing effect of those hundreds of hard battering rams thrusting away at them, the glimpses of possible friendship with the men, the shallow contact ... and, of course, the money, the independence.'

'My grandmother wanted me to take it up.'

'She's incorrigible.'

'Or honest. She says it's the finest possible life.'

'But you wanted none of it, *hein?*'

I laughed. 'You know me! I want and I don't want all at the same time. But if I had wanted it, I wouldn't have relished any of those things you mentioned. None of that would ever excite me. I some-

times used to daydream about it, after she raised the possibility. I liked to imagine myself waking up in the morning, with my oyster still tingling from last night's exercises, and I'd think, there's M Leblanc the merchant from near Vincennes, driving into Paris trying to think about his day's work and trying to ignore the pressure building up down there in his trousers ... and there's M Leclerc getting onto his omnibus at Bastille, his mind leaping over a long, boring day on his high stool and already trying to put a name, a figure, a fragrance to the girl who will take the gift of his lust that night ... and there's M Lefèvre whose wife has been called away and whose servants are old and ugly and who's never been with a Lady of Pleasure in his life but who's decided at long last ... et cetera. I'd think up six different men – men of business, or officers, artists, actors, impecunious students with their begging, adoring eyes – all as different as I could make them. And I'd lie there thinking to myself, here it is, ten o'clock in the morning, and all those six men are out there somewhere, building up a towering lust – a present for me – and though none of them even knows my name at the moment, this wonderful civilization of ours will somehow infallibly arrange for them to come to my door, take off my clothes, adore my sweet young body, make me their *petits cadeaux* of desire and skill and money – of which, of course, I would take full advantage. And then they'd go away and never bother me again until the next time!'

He laughed in delight at my fantasy and asked, 'What will you tell the Countess this time?'

'That I have all the *grands cadeaux* of desire and skill I could possibly want, in this one man – and something much more important than money. Have no fear, my darling. She won't do it to you again.'

Actually, I will tell my grandmother something more prosaic than that. I will say that I am just beginning to glimpse an important difference between what we wish to do in fantasy and what we actually do in reality. When I was fourteen I used to daydream endlessly about being raped; in my mind it was the most exciting thing ever. But even then I knew I would be horrified if it actually happened, even if my dream attacker turned into my real-life one. He was a young Adonis with vine leaves in his hair and the wild, overpowering reek of a goat.

Here's my grandmother now. I see her carriage coming up the Champs Élysées. What a grand figure she is still!

How can I even begin to summarize it all? Impossible. She was here five hours, talking to the Duke as much as to me. I'm sure he was under her spell once upon a time. When he was twenty she would have been thirty, two years before she met the Comte again and married him (and 'retired,' she says – ha ha!); she was certainly working in Paris at that time, one of the highest ranking courtesans of her day. She could have captured him then. The odd thing is, now we both know (the Duke and I) that the other knows she's my grandmother, I cannot ask him about his affaire, if any, with her! It borders on a kind of incest.

And so what of my grandmother? No, I cannot possibly summarize one tenth of the wisdom that fell from her lips during that time. Never mind the Duke, *I* am under her spell now! Does it matter if I cannot record it all in one fell swoop? No, I think not. Her words were like seeds; I will remember them when I eat the fruit and see the new seed ready to sow. I can record it then. Let me now write down such snippets as I have time for.

First she was not in the least angry that I had completely ignored all her carefully laid plans for my sentimental education; she claims she would have thought far less of me had I meekly fallen in with everything she suggested. She said the Duke was an even better mentor for me in sexual matters than Count François would have been …

ME: For one thing, we're not related! From your letters there would appear to be a chance that either Count, father or son, is my real grandfather.

Her nostrils flared at that, but it taught her I am independent of her now, and intend to remain so; when I say I am under her spell, I do not mean that I have become her creature. Not at all.

I added that I would never have been a Lady of Pleasure anyway.

COUNTESS: You should not say that, my dear. It is something every pretty young girl with strong appetites should try, if only for a single night. In classical times, before the Christians arrived with their darkness, every girl was a holy prostitute for a season. We were honoured then, as we should be now.

ME: But what could I learn in one of your houses that I cannot discover in more pleasant ways now?

COUNTESS: You should try it. Then you'd understand.

ME: If I did, I'd arrive on a day of my own choice, I'd pick the customers I liked, and I'd leave when I felt like it. I must always feel free to say no.

COUNTESS: Then, naturally you'll learn nothing.

ME: Such as? I can't imagine what learning you're talking about.

COUNTESS: The absolute control of your own ... what can I call her? Mr Raines says you laugh when I say Miss Laycock.

ME: *Vagin?*

COUNTESS: [*shuddering*] Very well. You will learn the absolute control of your own *vagin*. When you spread yourself out for a man who physically disgusts you and make him feel he has pleasured you royally, *then* you may hold your head high and shout to the rooftops, 'I control my own body!' If you confine yourself to those who please you from the start, you are little more than a slut. Besides, your *vagin* will pick from the same narrow range of men again and again. But when you cannot choose, when you must take those who choose you, then your mind is disengaged and you are truly free to study the innermost nature of male desire at work – then you will truly learn about men and their *flêches d'amour*.

I saw the Duke nodding sagely, and a little sadly, at the truth of all this. Later, when he tactfully left us alone, I told her how he was increasingly harping on this theme that I ought to go out and gather new experiences. She agreed with him. I told her of my adventures across the road at Vallodon's. She said she would be very interested to hear what became of the de la Tour incident; she was sure I hadn't seen the last of *that* fellow.

COUNTESS: Vallodon's condition is all in his mind, you know. He could easily get himself properly stiff and roger away ... I suppose you don't say roger, either?

ME: Pleasure away? From Lady of Pleasure, you see?

COUNTESS: [*sighing*] He could poke away all night still if he were treated in the right way.

ME: What way would that be?

COUNTESS: If I tell you, you must promise never to reveal it to another soul – or not casually, anyway. Only to someone you absolutely trust. And you must never, never write it down.

ME: Where did you learn it?

COUNTESS: I was told it by the Marquis de Q. on his most recent visit to France. It involves rings made of coconut fibre, but I have found one can use gutta-percha instead, and it's probably a little safer. He saw the technique used in the Tahitian islands as a way of killing rapists. They die at the very peak and climax of their ecstasy – so you see how dangerous it is.

As she made me promise to write nothing of it down, I omit all details here. The important thing is that the man must want it, otherwise it doesn't work – or is just a rather ordinary experience for him.

ME: Are Vallodon's girls really *la crème de la crème?* I have never actually met one of them yet.

COUNTESS: [*smiling*] You are looking at one now, my precious. Yes! I was one of his girls, from the age of twenty-five to the age of twenty-eight. They are mounted by only one or two lovers a day, you know, which is why they can be so good at it. The quieter pace of life suited me then, after my ranting and roaring days in London.

ME: And after that? Until you met the Comte again at thirty-two?

COUNTESS: Then I could afford to set up on my own. I took a villa in the Faubourg St Honoré and gathered around me my own circle of rich lovers and beautiful lovers and sweet young lovers ... and was very happy, until the dear Comte came back into my life and showed me what true happiness is.

ME: You mean owning the largest string of brothels and *maisons de tolérance* in Europe?

COUNTESS:[*smiling*] Wait until you are my age, *ma petite!*

That is all I have time to record today. I see a hot, urgent, one-eyed beggar edging towards me across my writing desk. I wonder? If I took my quill and wrote ever so tenderly on it the fact that I

[*Here in the manuscript is a blot and several angry smudges.*]

Wednesday 2nd November
That was not a good idea! Now he has shown me *where* to put the nib if I should ever again have such a crazy idea as to write love poems on a grown man's organ. And I have kissed it better almost all night.

I forgot to say that the Countess told me the Comte will never permit her to publish those letters to me. So poor little Raines has gone away in a huff. But the Comte cannot live for ever, and I believe they ought to be published. I did not tell her so, however.

Tonight is to be my final night at Vallodon's. He has promised me quite a different partner, but, after de la Tour I cannot raise that little thrill of excitement inside me.

I hear that new siren song: *A Lady of Pleasure For Just One Night!* I wonder if I shall ever sing it in earnest or is it like my daydream of rape?

Thursday, 3rd October.

Sic Transit Gloria Vallodonis! I have spread my thighs to a man for Vallodon's pleasure for the last time. But what a man! A Russian prince built like a bear. He must have weighed twenty stone – nearly three hundred pounds! And it was all solid muscle and hair and bone. Thank God his organ was not equally huge. I would have died; it was big enough as it was.

First he let me climb all over him, which was one of the most thrilling experiences ever, like having my own mountain of male flesh to scale and explore. But when he turned me over and lay on top of me – oooh! I could not believe it. I thought I would surely die. And then I found I was not dying but that he was inside me and moving in and out with the slowest, most delicate rhythm – maddeningly slow, tantalizingly, sweetly, beautifully slow. And absolutely regular. It was a slow, sure ride into a *plaisir* that set the bed on fire beneath me.

Poor Vallodon cried out in time with us both and I think enjoyed his finest climax in years. I was astonished to notice some stiffness lingering there in his *goujon*, even a minute later, when Bearski rolled off me and the cold air rushed in to kiss away my perspiration. Perhaps my Russian had heard about my contretemps with de la Tour, or maybe he never knew a girl who could take more than one tumble like that with him. Anyway, he thanked me and left.

I was just about to get dressed when Vallodon said to me, 'The other night, Mademoiselle Fanny, with de la Tour, I found it vastly stimulating. You are a most astonishing young woman.'

'On the bed here?' I asked.

'No, no. Afterwards, when you left him standing – literally, indeed, but in the wrong passage!'

I was about to say so much for Mme Laroche's pledge of secrecy when I remembered that our argument had taken place at the door of the octagonal room; he could have spied on us through his china cabinet. So I changed the subject. 'Monsieur Vallodon,' I asked him, 'do you truly wish you could have your powers restored to you?'

'Ah … *ma petite!*' He fondled me tenderly.

'Because I believe I know a way it might be done. Have you any elastic bands?'

Intrigued, he sent for this equipment.

I wish I had not promised I should never make a written record of this amazing technique. All I can say is that after fifteen gruelling minutes, when I was just beginning to think I must retire in a profusion of apologies and spend the next months wondering how I could make it up to him for his humiliation, his *baton* began to swell! I did as my grandmother had described with the elastic bands and the swelling grew urgent and very demanding. Vallodon's delighted eyes were popping out of his head.

I have seen the Duke's erection look as if it were close to bursting, what with so much fiery blood pumping through it, but that was nothing like this. Eager not to waste it or risk its falling away again, I took it deep into my mouth. But he jerked out and said, 'No no – you. I want you.'

He was standing, with me kneeling before him. I saw how close to coming he was so I jumped up, turned around, and offered myself to him that way. Moments later he was inside me and pumping away like a mad thing, as if he had not already spent copiously enough that night – crying out in such a mighty ecstasy that half the household came running: Mme Laroche, two of his courtesans who were pleasuring men in the house that evening, his secretary M Lebon, and several footmen and maids. And when they saw the miracle that was happening and heard him cry out that I was the Queen of Love – 'Elle est la Reine d'Amour! La Reine d'Amour!' – they could only stand and stare. And then, spontaneously, they all burst into applause!

But in the middle of it all, poor Vallodon fell at my feet, frothing and gasping. In the pandemonium that followed I managed to remove the elastics, which I slipped on his fingers instead.

Five minutes later he was sitting half up in bed, looking more like Voltaire's death mask than ever, and writing a codicil to his will. He had lived, he said, only to find someone to whom he could pass on his enterprise – and tonight he had found her. His previous pensions to his servants and certain friends were to stand, but the rest was to go to Mlle the Hon. Frances Duplessis, protégée of the Duc de R.

When it was signed and witnessed, everyone congratulated me and it was taken for granted that I would be passing the rest of the night in the old fool's bed. No, I must not be harsh like that – but what he did *was* utterly foolish, and I told him so, even while they were all about me. I told them not to be swept up in his madness but to try and make him see sense by morning, at which time they could tear up the whole stupid document.

I think that those who manage prostitutes and brothels seem to need a very special kind of mentality. They have to be utterly cold and commercial in matters of romance – and so, to balance the whole thing out, they must be utterly romantic and silly in matters of commerce.

Vallodon was not at all dismayed at my response. He said my good sense would reassert itself when the moment was right. Then he discovered my elastic bands around his fingers and he looked at me and laughed. 'Do not worry, mam'selle Fanny!' He shook them in the air for all the company to see. 'Your secret is safe with me!' And so it has proved. For now it *is* morning and they have just let me know M Vallodon died as the dawn came up.

So I now own, if that is the word, the twelve most desirable prostitutes in Paris. What on earth am I to do with them? I must send word to the Countess.

 Is this madness never to end? No sooner has the Duke finished laughing at my predicament than I have a note sent in from young de la Tour. It is the most craven apology a man of his spirit has ever written, I feel sure. How can I ignore something so utterly beautiful and disarming?

I go down to receive him and he falls at my feet to tell me he has at last found the perfect way to make his apology. I wave the letter and tell him it will do, it is more than enough. I am about to ask him if he desires another assignation with me (at the thought of which my other mouth is already drooling) when he says, 'Come with me, I will show you.'

The Duke says I must go, so I do.

De la Tour takes me to a house in the Faubourg St Honoré, where, as my grandmother had intimated, all the greatest courtesans live and breathe heavily. We stop outside one of the finest villas of them all. I think to myself: If this is an apology for taking my availability for granted, it's beginning to take a distinctly odd turn. But my *vagin* says shut up and let him get on with it.

He waves a hand up the wistaria-clad walls, taking in the romantic turrets, the delicate iron balconies, the lace-curtained windows, the tumbled profusion of slate roofs. 'What do you think of it?' he asks.

I tell him I think it is one of the most beautiful villas I ever saw. 'It's yours,' he says – just like that: 'It's yours.' I laugh and tell him he's sweet but he's not to play such tricks. 'Come and look at it,' he says.

We wander from room to room, all exquisitely furnished. And he keeps insisting it really is mine. At length I have to tell him that my body has called me every name under the sun for treating him as I did, that I am aching for him now, and that if he doesn't do something to quench my longing I'll ... I *just* manage to stop myself from saying 'die.'

He goes all stiff (in the wrong way, alas) and formal with me. He has not made me a gift of this house for that reason. He wants nothing in return. He demands nothing of me – that is the whole point of it. The villa is mine and I may order him out of it this instant and tell him never to see me again, and he will obey, happily, for then he will know he has restored my honour – and thus his honour, too.

I have no way of attacking such absurdity, so I sign the deed that is awaiting us, along with a notary, in the drawing room.

The notary goes.

I turn to him. 'You demand nothing,' I said. 'But if something is offered – with all the sweetness and humility, not to say desperation, I possess – then will you churlishly spurn it? Will you ignore a poor maiden in such dire distress?'

'What exactly is this offer of yours?' he asks, smiling that supercilious smile of his.

'You may start by blowing smoke rings all over my naked body. That recreation could develop in all sorts of interesting directions, I think.'

So now I have this tiger by the tail. I would never have believed such raw, rampant sexuality could be concealed in such an urbane, honour-obsessed body. Nothing is wasted in him. He has no finesse, no small talk, no humour, no shame – not once he starts. He is an utterly dedicated, tireless, demanding, pleasure-seeking, absolutely selfish, unbelievably fantastic lover. When he grabs me with those brutal, gentle hands and moves me, this way, that way – always brusquely, always with absolute fixity of purpose – I live in a whole cloud of climaxes. He is the all-night man who denies me the chance of being an all-night woman, though I can milk any other man ... well, I was going to say six feet under.

November 20th – Sunday.
Now I know the world is mad! Where can I go? What can I do? Every man in Paris, it seems, wants to dice with death. *La Gloire de Vallodon* is on everyone's lips. And the girl who pleasured to death the lucky man who owned the twelve most sought-after fillies in Paris ... well! She must be something quite out of this world, eh? Twenty thousand pounds sterling – which is around a hundred and forty

thousand francs! – has been offered me for a night of bliss between my thighs – and, to be sure, the learning of my secret. Oh, there are some astute men, here! For at those rates even so vast an outlay could be recovered in a week by passing this imaginary 'secret' on. Fortunately the Countess has agreed to take over Vallodon's enterprise; but I have made her agree that she is only my agent and that her only management fee is to be the ten percent that was all Vallodon ever took from the girls – and all the household expenses are to be met out of it.

It was a hard bullet for her to bite but the honour of 'owning' such a stable was too great for her to turn down. Both she and the Duke say I must get away from Paris until this nine-day-wonder has passed – about two months, they think. De la Tour has offered to take me to Venice. A whole month of that exhausting, dedicated pleasuring? Can I stand it?

[*Whatever passed between Young Fanny and de la Tour, whose first name we never learn, in Venice or elsewhere, must be left to our imagination. Neither in the published book nor the family archive is there any record of it. However, she and her vagina seem to have survived the experience. The Christmas of that year has her back in the villa, entertaining the Duke and de la Tour with equal frequency and fervour. Again, though, she merely records the fact of it; saying nothing of what they do or what she has learned during that time away. Her main preoccupation now seems to be with the decoration of her new home. There are pages and pages that have nothing to do with her sentimental education, and which I have therefore omitted. Her re-entry into her sexual life, or the recording of it in these pages, begins in a most unusual way with the unrolling of a new carpet for her bedroom in the villa. – FR]*

Thursday, 19th December, 1850.

The carpet finally arrived today and it turned out to be the most horrid thing imagineable. When they told me it had been bought of a Turkish merchant called Neroni Bey, who had made himself one of the richest men in France by importing the finest carpets and rugs from all over North Africa and the Orient, and that he was in Paris at that very moment, I thought I would play a splendid trick on him. True, Cleopatra had done it before me, but that was a long time ago and I felt the joke could stand another airing.

First I decided to dress as Salome, all ready to do the Dance of the Seven Veils; but then I thought no, that was rather obvious. The person Neroni Bey would least expect to come tumbling out of his returned creation – if he suspected anyone at all, that is – would be a dainty and proper young English girl, just left school. So that is how I dressed.

I do not recommend the interior of a carpet as a mode of transport, especially if it is a large one, as this was. The Bey's servants proved bribable, but even so they cautioned us to wait until the meal was drawing to its close. Another thing I do not recommend to any young female is that she should burst in upon a formal dinner given by a Turkish Bey in that way – even if it is drawing to its close. He was furious! I could hear him ranting and roaring even

76

through all that layering of wool and silk. And the process of unrolling so large a carpet in haste was something I had not considered, for I had been rolled into it at much greater leisure. My head was spinning by the time the final turn came, and several of those men must have thought me drunk as I tried to sit up.

During all this I heard the Bey's anger turning to laughter. But that was not my plan; I did not want to turn from complainant into clown, just to mollify his anger. 'Mr Neroni Bey,' I cried out sharply, trying to focus my eyes on at least one of that sea of whirling, distinguished faces. 'This is surely the vilest carpet you have ever had the temerity to sell to a lady of discrimination in the whole of your career in France!'

I found him then, staring down at me with such an amused disdain. The one thing they had omitted to tell me was that Neroni Bey was as black as an Ethiop. Oh, but he was beautiful! He was like one of those black leopards, sleek and deadly. Once you saw him you could not – dared not – take your eyes off him. He radiated that same sort of menace. His forehead was smooth and sleek; his nose was thin and aristocratic with little flares to his nostrils (which reminded me – I don't know why – of a perfect little pair of tight, firm, male buttocks); and his lips, though thin, were chiselled and sensuous. His firm chin, his high, delicate cheekbones, and his huge earlobes hinted at determination – a regal authority that was somehow different from that same quality in a European. There was some dangerous, exciting *otherness* about him. I thought he could hardly be more than twenty years old, though, from his business success, he must be at least twenty-five.

All this I took in in a flash. No, even to say I 'took it in' is false. I felt it like a revelation. He saw it, too. Between one chuckle and the next he saw that desperate revaluation going on behind my eyes, and it changed his whole perception of me, in turn. He saw at once through my English Rose disguise to that old, familiar craving which was already working its magic within me.

Whatever protest he had been about to make suddenly deserted him and he said, instead, 'You are quite right, mam'selle. It is a most indifferent carpet. However, in my own defence I feel compelled to add that they told me it was for a young courtesan who flatters herself she is Aphrodite's gift to the manhood of France – though, or so they assured me, she is, in fact, most feebly endowed. They said I should do her an immeasurable favour if I supplied a carpet whose insipidity would offer only the smallest competition to her sallow complexion, her skinny body, and her utterly picayune taste in art and ornament.'

A great gasp went up from his guests. Every eye turned upon me. So there was my test! Would I wither under the heat of his scorn, or could I prove myself worthy of ... closer inspection?

Still sitting in the middle of that awful rug, I crossed my knees and spread out my great crinoline dress demurely. 'Sir,' I told him quietly, 'the blind and otherwise defective courtiers with whom you have obviously *chosen* to surround yourself is a matter of indifference to me, and I think it odd you should complain to me in person about their opinions *of* that person when the clash must be plain to a sightless idiot. Or have you grown so feeble in your own observation that you must now rely entirely on the self-serving lies of these numskulls?'

It seemed to take about ten seconds for his smile to grow from the merest twitch at the corners of those superb lips to the broadest and most masterful grin. I had not only passed the test, I had set him a challenge he could not now refuse. 'Mam'selle,' he said, in a tone that lacked the slightest degree of sincerity, 'I owe you at least a partial apology.'

'Partial?' I echoed.

He waved a hand toward me. 'To your face, which I now confess is as beautiful as any I have ever seen, I apologize unreservedly. To your delicate hands, which are like the rarest of our desert blossoms, what can I give but my abject apology? And – yes! – from one glimpse of an ankle that is surely without equal in this hemisphere – from that, too, I crave forgiveness.'

And his eyes said the rest, roving over my clothing, undressing me where I sat. I could almost feel myself being peeled by him. My heart began to flutter. My breath grew short. I had no hope of negotiating another fine speech. He smiled and, glancing around the table, said, 'Gentlemen?'

They knew a hint when it came with a fog-horn. Moments later we two were alone together. I loved the radiance of power that just poured out from him. I began to stand up but he laid his fingertips gently on my head. 'That is the right way to sit on a carpet, Mam'selle Duplessis. Even one as execrable as that. So you are right. It is the vilest I have ever sold. I scoured two continents to find it.'

'But why, Monsieur ...?'

'Call me Nero.' He sat down, cross-legged, and faced me. Our knees were almost touching. 'Have you any idea how unreachable you are these days? What chance had I, a poor, humble carpet seller, standing in that long, desperate line of would-be suitors? No, I had to choose a carpet of such appalling taste that your anger would not simply reject it, but actually bring you to me. But I hardly expected' – he moved his hands apart in benediction – 'this magnificence.'

I swallowed heavily.

'And now it has done its work so well,' he said, moving toward me, lifting his delicate, teasing fingers to my bodice hooks, 'should we not reward it with the knowledge, the glow of satisfaction, that for all its tawdry beastliness, it nonetheless had its one hour of glory, when it made a bed for the two greatest lovers of their day?'

I can honestly say that I have never seen – nor imagined nor dreamed of – anything so magnificent as his naked black body. He had not an ounce of puckered skin, and he was burnished like the finest ebony, from his forehead to his ankles. He had nipples like small black peas, which went on fire when I stroked or sucked them. His stomach was flat and smooth, and firm as a board – a perfect resting pad for an organ that almost made me fall apart in my delight, just to see it. It was long and hoisted itself aloft in a wicked, scimitar-like curve. He had been circumcised perfectly, so that when he was as hard and imperative as this, all the slack skin was taken up, covering a throbbing, black, gristle-hard rod on which a beautiful, pale bronze knob quivered and begged for the snug, warm darkness.

His body had a smell unlike any other man's – not that I had known many, but this was so different it put him in a class apart. It was acrid and musky and drowsy and strong. It filled me with obscure commands that I could not choose but to obey. And the taste of his *fusil* when I took it in my mouth was all of that musky strength, ten times more concentrated.

And yet it is not these physical things I remember best. I dwell on them because they were the most immediately obvious differences between my pleasuring with him and with any other man. But what lingers with me now is the feeling – at the time it was more than that, it was like a religious conviction – that he had found some way of uniting his nervous system with mine. I have felt that before with the Duke, and, to a degree, with de la Tour; but in their case I felt it merely allowed us to know, with a wonderful immediacy, what was happening inside each other's turmoil. With Nero it was much more.

It wasn't that he simply knew what was happening inside me – he *was* what was happening inside me. Obviously that was true in the purely physical, sexual sense, but I mean it in an erotic, emotional way, as well. He was my heartbeat; his sweetness was every breath I inhaled; his fire was my blood; and at the last his exhaustion became my slumber.

When I awoke – next morning, and we were in his bed by then, though I have only the vaguest recollection of waltzing thither, impaled on that magnificent black wand – when I awoke, I was tied to this man in ways I could never begin to describe.

Is it love?

I honestly do not know. It is like nothing I have ever felt before. Somewhere deep inside me I now have the profoundest conviction that this man's destiny and mine are henceforth linked together. That is not something flowery I have worked out since; I knew it instantly, the moment I awoke and smelled that beautiful, lean, black body, which was still entangled in mine. Obviously our sexuality is at the heart of it, but it goes out far beyond. All of him and all of me are now held in that same tight bond.

I looked down at him fondly; I think I can love men most tenderly at times like that, when I awaken before them and study their faces in repose. Then they seem at their most vulnerable and boylike, and something of the mother in me cannot help but respond. But, as I suddenly realized, there was none of that with Nero. Even in sleep that black leopard lay coiled within him; it still had the power to force my heart up into my throat, where it beat a little faster. There were intimations of selfishness and cruelty – part of that powerful otherness of his – in those gently closed eyes, those peaceful lips.

He did not wake until they brought us breakfast. I wanted to spend the morning in bed, renewing all our last night's joys, but he said he was a man of affairs and I would have to wait.

And I did not explode in indignation!

'Actually,' he said, throwing himself languidly back against the pillows, 'let us talk of affairs.'

'Mine or yours?'

'Perhaps both ...' And he went on to explain how, although Turkish by birth, he was from Abyssinian parents – rich merchants who had been bankrupted in a swindle perpetrated by the Sultan's chief eunuch. The eunuchs were always the power behind the Turkish throne, so the man was untouchable. But Nero Bey (his real name – he only uses Neroni in Europe because of the unfortunate association with the Roman emperor here) had made a good marriage at twenty, and had put his wife's dowry to most practical effect. For the past ten years (so he was now thirty!) he had scoured the bazaars and markets of the orient, buying up carpets that he was sure would suit the European taste. That was his forte – a profound, almost uncanny, awareness of European taste. By now he was far and away the biggest carpet merchant in Europe, with offices in every large city.

'But the Orient cannot keep up with me,' he said. 'Now I have my own trained agents in the bazaars but they cannot find enough. And you can't tell those orientals what to do. They only say, "No, this is the way Allah wills it." Aieee!'

'You should set up your own factory,' I told him.

He sat bolt upright and stared at me in horror. 'Who have you been talking to?'

'You!' I laughed. 'If that isn't the point of your story, then I've completely misheard you.'

Then, with one of those astounding changes of mood, which cuts right into the heart of me, his whole face softened and he took my head between his loving hands and kissed me. 'You will take some getting used to,' he murmured.

'Will I?' I gasped.

'Listen – or have you already guessed?'

'I don't want to try. Just tell me – but quick.'

'For the next year or so my wandering days are over. My palace is not, in fact, in Turkey but in Sidi-el-Barrès in Tunisia – because of my enormous French connections, you see. So there I shall sit for the next twelve months and build my carpet factory and train my loom minders ... and I will make the carpets Allah does not will from the orient.'

'And you will need a female companion,' I said.

'A concubine.'

Now it was I who sat bolt upright.

'Indeed,' he nodded. 'What did you think? I do not live in the sort of community where I could put you in an apartment and come visiting every afternoon. You will live – I beg your pardon – *if* you do me this inestimable honour and agree to become my concubine – you will live in honourable estate in the harem with my wife and the slaves.'

I laughed. 'And a eunuch, I'm sure!'

He nodded mildly. 'Of course. His name is Bulbull. Everything is impeccably correct, as you'll see.'

I lay back and fanned myself. 'I don't know, Nero. Let me think it over. Can I answer tomorrow?'

'No.'

'You mean I have to decide now?'

'Yes.'

'Then I'm sorry, I must say no.'

He made no move whatsoever; he just stared at the ceiling with a knowing smile on his lips.

'Your wife,' I said. 'What would she think about it?'

'She will be glad of the company.'

'Yes, but you know what I'm talking about.'

'Sex? She won't mind that. We no longer enjoy those sort of relations. I love her very proudly, but that is outside our understanding with each other.'

'And is it her choice, too – this continence?'

'Naturally. I am not a tyrant.'

'And have you any other concubines?'

'No. There would have been no point until now – since I'm hardly ever home. I can easily get some more if you want.'

'Of course I don't want! But would you get some anyway – whether I wanted it or not?'

'If you satisfied me entirely, then I wouldn't. But the decision is mine. I will not bind myself now.'

'You'd have to, or I wouldn't come.'

'Then don't come.'

I sighed. '*Alors,* I'll stay in Paris, thank you.'

Then I asked, 'What about the slave girls?'

'I have only two in the harem. They're both about fifteen years old. One will soon be sixteen – but too young yet to unite their bodies with me.'

'Why do you have them there then?'

'There is no need for you to know that unless you accept my offer. Then you'll see for yourself. I ... they were going to die. I rescued them. I gained merit by it and one day they will make beautiful concubines, perhaps even wives. Allah is merciful.'

'And that's your entire harem? A wife and two slaves – with all of whom you live in celibacy?'

'And perhaps the most beautiful concubine any man could wish for? Harem life has moved on since the days of Lady Mary Wortley Montagu. You will find it more like living in a grand Parisian hotel. I have the finest library in Tunisia; we take all the Parisian papers and any magazines or ladies' journals you may care to order. You can go on shopping expeditions, attend public lectures, the theatre, the opera ... all the things you have no time for here!'

I was, of course, already persuaded – even had I to live in purdah with this magical man. One question remained: 'What would be your contribution to the years when that beauty no longer shines?'

'You may set that price,' he said. 'Let me warn you – do not cheapen yourself for me. I could buy up your Duke and M de la Tour several times over.'

'You're taking a risk, Nero,' I warned him archly. 'After the unfortunate M Vallodon expired between my thighs, I was bid up to twenty thousand pounds sterling for a single night of bliss.'

He nodded. 'And you turned it down, I hear?'

'Because the offers were quite absurd. Venus herself could not possibly be worth so much.'

He reached over to the bedside cabinet and opened a drawer. From it he took a piece of paper, which he at once passed to me. It was a bill of exchange, drawn up in my favour and made payable at sight, for 22,222 English guineas. [*In 1980s currency that is worth over a million pounds, sterling – FR*] 'Is her nearest representative on Earth worth so much for a year?' he asked.

I was too flabbergasted to utter a word. At my cheekiest I might have asked for a quarter of that.

'Understand one thing,' he went on. 'This money has been yours from before you entered this house. It is not payment for anything – not the joys of last night, not the infinite joys that await us in the harem during the year ahead. It is yours whether you agree to become my concubine or not.'

'But if I do agree, then it must become a kind of payment,' I objected.

'Not at all. It is there to prevent you from worrying – to relieve you of all worries of that kind. It is there to free you – to make you free to do the one thing you have consented to do.'

'When did you draw it up?' I had to ask.

'The day I sold your steward that carpet. And now I really must rise, dear Fanny.'

I lay there and curled up deliciously around the thought – as I watched him dress – that those two gorgeous black buttocks would soon be mine, thrusting so firmly, so urgently, to make me explode ... and that long, limp gristle would soon ... 'One more thing?' I asked. 'Why is it all written in twos?'

'Because they look like swans – and you, with your pale elegence and your statuesque grace, remind me of a swan.'

He never said a single wrong thing. Immediately after Christmas I sail for Tunisia and my new life in the harem! The Duke has sadly consented – and now that he has I may safely say that I would not otherwise have gone.

Me – a concubine! I can't believe it even now.

Wednesday, January 1st, 1851.

An appropriate day on which to start a new life. Not the best of beginnings, though – no Nero to meet me at the quayside. Instead there was Yussuf, his vizier, who is as trustworthy as a wooden firetongs, I'd say. But I bucked up on seeing our palace – a large Parisian hotel was not a bad description. Downstairs was full of people who would not believe the Bey was away; everyone wants favours. Slaves went before me and beat a path among the crowds using vicious, whippy sticks called 'scorpions,' which sting like their namesakes but leave no bruise. Everyone scampered out of the way and fell prostrate before me. I told Yussuf I didn't like it; he replied that I soon would. 'Soon you will like everything here.' It gave me an uneasy feeling for he said it more like a command than a promise.

But I certainly liked my accommodation, which is more like a hotel *suite* than a single room. I curtseyed very low before Sulayah, Nero's wife. He had asked me to show her such formal respects. In fact, he need not have bothered; I would have done so anyway. She has such immense grace and dignity, and her eyes are so placid and understanding. She earned my respect at once. The one curiosity is that there is no bed anywhere. I did not want to ask why. Perhaps my bed is to be in Nero's room, even when he is away. I am writing this down swiftly, before I forget it. Soon we will have lunch and I will meet the two little slave girls, who will assist in preparing me for *his* return! And then ... ah, then, who knows what?

I know what! God, shall I ever be able to walk again? Nero is not, as it happens, coming home tonight, but there would be no point, anyway; I am just numb down there. The two little slaves, Sherry (from Scheherazade) and Salome – both names being given them by Nero – are from India, the Mussulman part, wherever that is. As soon as they undressed me for my bath, Sulayah stared at me in horror. She had never seen a woman who had kept her pubic hair before – nor the hair beneath her arms, nor the line of it up her belly. She said something in Arabic to the two little girls and they ran off into the harem, where I next heard the screech of a rope and pulleys. Sulayah led me back, clucking in annoyance and holding me tight, as if she thought I might stumble; obviously, with all that hair, I was a very sick person in their eyes.

The pulleys had been used in order to lower an ornately carved and gilded frame, which now lay flat on the floor – rather like a big picture frame in the rococo style, eight feet square, but without any canvas or looking glass to fill it. That role was to be mine, for she invited me to lie down within that ornate square. And I – God forgive my innocence – I, remembering my early weeks with the Duke, thought I was about to be photographed already framed! This exciting female oddity with actual hair! I complied, of course, and eagerly.

Even when Sulayah grabbed me by one wrist, and Bulbull (this was my first introduction to him) leaped out from nowhere and seized the other, I still did not guess. I do not like the look of Bulbull at all – a fat, sleek man with the skin of an oily woman; he exuded a positive hatred of me from the very outset; indeed, it is a hatred of all women, for even Sulayah gets accorded only the most grudging and surly respect.

The two little slaves had meanwhile, and without my knowing it, contrived to bind my ankles to their end of the frame. I was too busy registering the fact that Bulbull and Sulayah were doing the same to my wrists at the top. So there I was, trussed like a letter X and framed in gold! And then those two little monkeys started their devilish work – Salome and Sherry, I mean. Bulbull just sat by and grinned at the fun; Sulayah took only an occasional hand in the business. And I screamed and yelled until I was exhausted. For what the little girls had done was to dip their hands in some kind of resin and then, feeling their way around my armpits, they plucked out each hair, and sometimes several, by the roots.

But the real horror of it was the sudden realization, as I stared at their mischievous little faces close up for the first time – that they were both quite blind! Their nimble, dark-skinned little fingers crawled over my pale skin like spiders; and when they felt a hair, no matter how small, they seized it and tweaked it out with a force that I would have thought beyond their delicate little fingers. And the more I screamed, the more they giggled.

The moment they had finished with my armpits, Sulayah applied an ointment – which, I have to allow, dulled the pain at once. Soon all I felt there was a rosy glow that was not even unpleasant. 'Why could you not have put that on first?' I asked.

'Because the oil would make their fingers slip,' she replied placidly. My pain moved her not at all; like childbirth, it was something women endured to please the men, and therefore themselves.

And then the two monkeys, their fingers rested, began on my pubic hair. Well, I thought I should die – especially when they began on the hairs that surrounded my labia, closest to my holey of holeys. But I was past screaming by now; I just lay still and moaned in pain.

'Nero will be furious,' I told her. 'He said he was so delighted with that hair in France.'

'In France he was,' she agreed. 'Things are different here. He is different here.'

When they had gone as far as they could, Bulbull turned the frame over – gently, I was pleased to note – and they finished off the hairs around my bottom. Then he turned me over again and the females massaged the ointment into my mound and all my tormented folds. I confess that one gentle and two childish hands working a soothing ointment into those places was … well, I am not one of those women, like my grandmother, who can find almost equal pleasure with another woman as with a man, yet I have to allow, it was more than pleasant.

Then they set me free and told me I could dress. Apparently I may wear European dress in the daytime, harem costume in the evenings, and I know not what at night. I still don't know where I am to sleep. They said there was no point in any further preparation for Nero Bey now, because I would take a day to heal. Privately I thought I would take a lot longer than that.

I will go down to the library and read the papers. Not that I am homesick, mind. I wish Nero were here, even with me like this.

'Harem costume' consists of a very fetching pair of silk trousers, gauzy and slightly revealing in my case, and a light velvet jacket that hangs loosely over my breasts, showing nothing except my navel. My hair is done elaborately by two very pleasant young slave girls from outside the harem – they make me wonder why Nero paid so much to have me come here, especially if there are more like those two down below. One has an especially delicate face and a very gentle manner. They had no French, so we could not converse much. I think I must learn Arabic.

After a supper whose cuisine was well up to anything I ever tasted in Paris, Sulayah turned to me and said, 'Bulbull will do the ritual now, if you wish. Perhaps you might like to get it all over and done with on the one day?'

Queasily I asked what this 'ritual' might be.

'The Six Marks of Submission,' she said, touching my arm sympathetically. 'I'll stay at your side. He will be as merciful as he dares, if I tell him.'

My heart was racing as I said, 'I'm sorry. I'm completely ignorant of all these things.'

'He will give you six strokes of the lash. One on each side of your back, one on each buttock, and one on each thigh. He is very accurate. I have seen some appalling slips in my time, but you need have no worry on that score.'

'But what's it for? What have I done to deserve it?'

She seemed to think it was a genuine question – and a hard one at that.

91

'You are a woman, I suppose,' she said, as if that were the only possible explanation. 'How else can we show our submission on entering Nero Bey's harem?'

'I'll put it in writing if you like.'

It had no meaning to her, not even as a joke – especially not as a joke.

'Do I have to?' I asked.

'Of course not – what an idea! Our master is no tyrant like that. He is the gentlest of men.'

'Yes, he told me so himself. Well then, I think I'll say pass to that particular custom.'

'It's your choice, of course. But you must understand that he cannot lie with you until you do.'

I smiled. 'Well, we'll see about that when he comes. What about the two little girls? Did they have to undergo it, also?'

'Good heavens! Don't you know anything? If a girl enters the harem before her bleeding starts, her submission is automatic.'

Bulbull was furious. I now have a triple-proof enemy there – and yet I feel so sorry for him, too.

Our sleeping arrangements have been made clear to me at last: We all sleep together! Our beds are arrangements of blankets and heavily stuffed palliasses on the harem floor – and silk sheets. Sulayah and I have a space each, about eight foot by six, bigger than any conventional bed I ever had. The two monkeys sleep in a similar space together. Our pyjamas are like men's – a tunic top and trousers at the bottom, all of the lightest, flimsiest, gauziest material. The drawstring of the trousers reaches only just around our hips, about two inches below the navel and the crotch of them is wide open, like women's drawers. The tunic ends about three inches below our breasts. There is no doubting that the true purpose of these costumes is to excite a man. One glance is enough. I felt so amorous the moment I put mine on that I would not have minded Nero coming back after all. Oddly enough the little monkeys wear the same night attire – to accustom them to their future life, I suppose. They are certainly quite shameless in their enjoyment of each other's sex; they were still giggling and making little whimpering sounds as I fell asleep.

Saturday, January 4th.

He is back! I will anticipate nothing. I will write it exactly as it happened. Perhaps then I shall come to believe it, too!

He came into the harem after our supper last night and we all greeted him with our varying styles of enthusiasm. He had a long, solemn talk with Sulayah first, during which I'm sure she told him about my refusal to accept the Six Marks of Submission. Then he took the two blind monkeys on his knee and heard all their lessons for the day.

The story of these fortunate-unfortunate girls is that they are from different but neighbouring families in the same quarter of Madras. They both went blind at around the same time; Sherry was then twelve or so, Salome thirteen. Their families had put them out on the streets to beg, where they would most probably have died. The Bey saw them. I no longer know what moral judgement to make of that man. Perhaps it was an act of genuine piety; perhaps he just needed to impress a big Indian supplier of carpets. And why not both – he is complicated enough for that, as I now know to my own chagrin.

Anyway, he purchased them as slaves and brought them to his harem here, four or five years ago. Now he insists on their having the best education and that they should learn all their feminine accomplishments. I think their schooling is far better than mine; they also sing, play the lute and mandolin, and dance. They entertained us for an hour last evening – and very well, too. The Bey was especially pleased, and his delight was obviously an enormous thrill to them.

Then he turned to me.

'Are you as desperate as I am?' I asked him.

'Sssh! We do not discuss such things in the harem.'

'Will I spend the night with you?'

'I won't tell you again.' He was angry now.

'You never said anything about these Six Marks of Submission in Paris.'

'I couldn't tell you every little thing. I assumed you were young enough – and your spirit big enough – to adapt to different customs. If I was wrong, that's a pity. Anyway, what does it amount to? Six lashes! You'd be healed in a week.'

'Hah! You only say that because it's not you who has to take these ridiculous stripes.'

He smiled at me and rose to his feet. 'Bulbull,' he snapped, not even checking to see the man was there. 'Go and fetch your whip, the one for females.'

Bulbull, thinking I had consented at last, ran to obey. When he returned, Nero said, '*I* will accept the Six Marks of Submission on this young lady's behalf. Do not be merciful.'

All this while he went on staring at me. I did not believe he would do it. I could not imagine anyone accepting the lash voluntarily like that. Right until that first awful crack resounded on his flesh, I thought it was a ruse.

And Nero did not flicker so much as an eyelid. It was I who cried out in my pain – and leaped behind him just in time to intercept the second lash. Oh my God – I thought it had cut me right in two! How could he not flinch? How could he just go on standing there with that superior smile on his face?

'Enough,' he told the eunuch quietly. 'She will now consider the matter.'

'Never!' I swore, sitting down again and rubbing my back hard, as if I could somehow flatten out the pain and share it with the unhurt flesh around. 'How could you take it without even flinching?' I asked.

He sat down beside me and spoke as if we were talking about the most mundane things in all the world. 'It is a matter of the will. You think my body is beautiful?'

'God, you know I do!'

'That is because it will do anything I ask of it. And it will obey because it has learned to trust me. Attitude is everything. One day it will all fall into place. Meanwhile, if you cannot yet see it, take my hand and trust me? Submit to me.'

I shook my head. 'I made a different bargain with you. There was no talk of any of this back in Paris. You can honour your original bargain or not. That's up to you.'

'Of course it is,' he said with that maddeningly lazy grin. 'It's entirely up to me. I'm pleased you can see that. There now – you've learned to take the first step already.' And then he spoke for another hour or so about his plans for the factory and the contracts he had won in Europe. Sulayah joined us at that stage and it ended with the two of them discussing designs in great detail.

And then he left us. That was it, I thought.

But then the slaves came in and cleared everything away. They made up our beds and undressed us hastily; there was a feeling of excitement in the air – as if we might not be ready when the Master came back. The two little slave girls could barely contain themselves; I wondered what their excitement could be all about? Were they allowed to watch Nero and me? I hoped not.

At about half past twelve, when I had almost given him up, he came back into the harem. The dim nightlight gleamed off his nakedness and when he stood over me I found myself looking directly up at that magnificent ebony rod, as proud and provoking as I'd ever seen it.

'Aaaah!' I gave out a long, gentle sigh and moved over to let him slip beneath the sheets at my side.

It was as if I were not there. He kicked at whichever of the two little girls was nearest me and said, 'Both of you – quick now!' and spun on his heel and left the chamber.

'Nero!' I called after him.

Sulayah sat up and frowned at me, waving her finger imperiously for me to be quiet. Sherry and Salome had meanwhile risen. Skipping and leaping like two little dervishes, they were taking fingerloads of lotion and rubbing it into and around their little, pink, hairless labia; Salome was also rubbing some into her tiny breasts.

I turned to Sulayah in horror. 'Surely not?' I whispered. 'He wouldn't do such a thing – just to teach me?'

She shook her head. '*They* will teach you,' she said gently. 'Come and see.' And she held out her hand. Her attitude seemed to be that she was doing me a great favour.

She took me to the wall beyond her bed, which was made up of elaborately pierced brick and faience. Until now I had taken this to be a mere decorative cladding to a solid wall beyond. But now, standing up and going close to it, I saw that the piercing gave a view into another chamber. And what a chamber!

The Room of Joys it is called. Lighted by a dozen small candles, which cast a warm, erotic glow, it was a profusion of carpets and silks and cushions and little padded stools of various heights. The air that wafted through to us was heavy with incense. I searched for the burner and there, so dark-on-dark I had not noticed him before, was Nero. He sat on a broad, padded stool, facing the door, and sideways on to us. His *poignard* was so stiff, so beautifully curved, so upstanding, that it almost entered his own navel. I felt sick with longing for him.

'See?' It was hardly even a whisper that Sulayah made with her lips so close to my ear.

And, indeed, I did. I saw the two little slaves entering the room. All their exuberance was held in check now. Their sightless eyes were downcast and they shuffled into the room toward him as if he, too, might have a whip. When they were close enough for Nero to reach, he leaned forward and put a hand in between the thighs of each, using his palms almost like two mighty platforms to lift them gently and hurry them forward onto his lap. And there they sat with their frail, birdlike thighs parted over his, the ointment on their moist labia polishing his magnificent muscles to the brightest gloss.

They did not move. They just sat there, breathing urgently, eyes closed, waiting. Sulayah at my side nodded approvingly, just as she had when they played some tricky passage on the lute with true feeling.

Nero murmured something to them and they took off their tunics, lifting them up over their heads. His gently outstretched fingers began to whisk with feather lightness over their bare chests, playing with their nipples, massaging their ribs, then turning over so that the backs of his knuckles ran down to their navels. They began to give out little moans and to breathe heavily, even to gasp; but their faces remained absolutely impassive. It was as if all the ecstasy were bottled so tight inside them that none could rise to play upon the surface, in their faces.

He shifted himself forward so that only the edges of his marvellous buttocks were on the stool; then he put his hands behind and hugged them to him, caressing their backs and slipping his fingers below their drawstrings to scratch their *derrières*. Now they moaned and sang their delight; but their faces were still entirely calm.

Nero called out something in Arabic. Sulayah turned and asked me if I had changed my mind. 'Never!' I told her angrily, suppressing the protests that swelled in the seething cauldron of my *vagin*.

When she relayed my refusal, he called out something else, which caused her to slip on a robe and leave the harem. He, meanwhile, stood up, hugging the little girls to him, and strode over to a deep bank of cushions, where he laid them down as tenderly as if they had been sleeping babes. They immediately drew up their legs and hugged their knees to their breasts, exposing two sweet, delicate, hairless little figs of flesh in the openings of their drawers – a carnal feast on which Nero now began to dine.

It soon became impossible for them to control their faces any longer. They whimpered and squirmed under the gentle, maddening assault of that most athletic of tongues. My own sweet fig – hairless herself now – remembered every ripple of it, every curl, every fold. I felt as if I were aching myself to bits as I watched all that skill being expended on them. Then Salome arched her back and raised her pelvis to grab at her thrills. 'Oh!' she cried, and 'Oh!' again, as if the surprise were completely virgin with each new wave of it. His finger, busy meanwhile on

Sherry's clitoris, was bringing her the like miracle.

But as soon as she came he spun himself on his back and she leaped on top of him, thighs straddling him, and rubbed herself into an absolute frenzy on the long back of his great, black *epée*. Measured by the intensity of her *plaisir,* she was the older, not the younger, of the two. Meanwhile, Salome squatted demurely over him and let him wind her down from plateau to plateau with his hands and tongue.

A sudden movement made me realize that Sulayah had returned – not to me but to that Room of Joys; she was leading by the hand one of the young slave girls who had helped me in the bath yesterday – I mean, the day before. She was clad in a single garment, a frail tube of cotton gauze with holes for her arms and a simple drawstring at her neck. It covered her down to her ankles, but there was no mistaking the size and beauty of her breasts, nor the swelling of her nipples. She did not even look at what was happening among the cushions just two paces away, but she was breathing hard and I could see her heartbeat shivering her breasts.

'Well?' Nero called out jovially to me.

'Never,' I spoke just loud enough for him to hear.

He patted the two little girls on their bottoms and they rose immediately to join Sulayah. The moment they were out of that room they came running to join me at the wall and watch the rest of the action – and, more especially, to watch me.

Hah! I wrote 'watch' quite unconsciously there. Those two monkeys are amazing. They 'see' things with their ears. They had as good a picture of what was happening in there as either Sulayah or me. Yet it must have been by hearing alone – unless by now they have developed some supernatural connections between them and their Master.

Nero rose and came back to the stool where I had first seen him sitting. He adopted his former position, too – side-on to me, facing the trembling slave girl; his *flêche d'amour* was as rock-hard as ever and was still upright against his stomach. He murmured something to the girl, who came and stood, her knees almost touching his, and waited once more.

He spoke again; she shook her head.

'He has just asked her if he has enjoyed her body before tonight,' Sulayah translated to me.

His next question was, 'Do you object if I enjoy you now?'

Briefly the girl stared down at him with her large, luminous eyes and joy lit up her graceful, flowerlike face. She could not speak; she simply shook her head.

'Is that another "Ritual"?' I asked sarcastically.

'In this household it is. Those women down there would fight each other for this privilege.'

'But could they actually refuse?'

'Of course. The Qura'n forbids a master to use his slaves sexually without their consent.'

Nero had meanwhile reached up and tugged at the drawstring around her neck. She shrugged her shoulders and the single garment fell from her. I was stabbed through with jealousy just to look at her. She was a brown-skinned Tunisian girl, though almost fair when set beside him. She, too, was plucked hairless and her mound gleamed from the unguent she had already rubbed in there – though, to judge by the excitement she had shown, the additional lubrication was hardly necessary. Her waist was slim but her hips swelled out in a most feminine way; and her breasts were fabulous – firm, plump, and with large, dark nipples, already engorged with pleasure.

Nero ran his hands up and down her body, watching her shiver. But her face had that same dreamy

100

impassivity I had seen in the two little monkeys. He caught her nipples between his thumbs and fingers and began to roll them gently; she stretched right up as far as she could, throwing back her head and thrusting them toward him. Yet still she had to maintain that fiction of her reticence, not moving onward to something new until he led her to it. I could not possibly imagine Fanny Duplessis holding herself back like that!

Those maddeningly gentle hands went down to her waist and turned her softly round until her pale *derrière* was before him. Now he devoted all his caresses to those two firm moons of her buttocks, slowly, slowly bringing her nearer him. Her knees were outside his thighs so that, as she moved backwards, her limbs were forced by the most gentle degrees ever farther apart. At last the knob of his *friandise* vanished between her parted thighs, but I knew it could not yet be touching her – and most especially that part of her which must now be craving the feel of him more than anything else in the world.

The sweat of anticipation was pouring off the girl. Between my own thighs I could feel the violence of my longing for that primal touch; it was bad enough for me, but she must have been driven almost out of her mind by it. At last his hands went up to her waist and gripped it firmly; simultaneously he spread his thighs wide apart, forcing hers to go even wider – and then he pulled her down on him. She gave out one great sigh of ecstasy, which was matched by the four of us beyond the wall.

He pulled her tight to him. One hand went down to her rosebud and the front of her labia, the other went up to her chest, extended wide so that thumb and little finger could work on both her nipples at once. I saw her arch her back, bending her *cul* to fit the beautiful banana-curve of his stupendous organ. He climaxed into her without moving, and she reached her mouth to the heavens, gasping every ounce of breath from her body at the sensation of that potent explosion inside her.

Rather soon after that he withdrew from her – and then I knew it was only a preliminary. He would now spread an entire feast for my jealousy to feed on. I turned away then, intending to go miserably to bed, but Sulayah tapped my arm and shook her head. Not to watch our Master at his pleasure – when he commands it – is a whipping offence anyway. (But, naturally, he is not a tyrant!)

'He is asking her if she would permit him to enjoy her again,' she told me.

'Goodness, what a surprise!' I replied.

The girl turned her sweetly shy smile on him and whispered no, she would deem it the greatest honour.

He asked her if there was anything he might do to increase her ecstasy. She blushed and lowered her head. He encouraged her to tell him, without coyness or fear, taking her into his hands and pulling her upon his lap. His erection was still almost as stiff as before. He put her hand to it and murmured something that even the two monkeys could not catch. She giggled, buried her face in her hands, and shook her head.

This was the ritual, of course – the reluctant, blushing female and the gentle but ruthless male, hunting out the orgiastic desires buried deep inside her, bringing them to the surface, making of them a gift to her who already owned them but who – without the magic of his body – could not discover them herself. Dear heavens – where is that marvellous creature with whom I spent the night in Paris? He is not here.

At long last, after a great deal more cajoling, and blushing, and hiding her face, and shaking her head, she took him by the hand and led him to a mountain of pillows almost at our feet. The angle of the pierced holes in the bricks prevented our seeing them there; I sighed with relief and prepared to go back to bed. But Sulayah told him of our difficulty. He said she and the two monkeys could go to bed; I was to join them in there.

I saw no point in arguing with him – in any case, my true opponent was not Nero but the lash of Bulbull's whip. I took Sulayah's gown, for I was damned if I was going to show my private parts to a slave girl in those circumstances, and went in. He smiled warmly and invited me to bring one of the smaller footstools and sit nearby.

The girl was most inventive! She simply lay on her back, thighs apart, knees slightly bent, and waited for him to lie on top of her. *Make this one interesting, if you can!* I challenged him in my mind.

He reached his hand up and rubbed my lips. 'Don't smile like that,' he said – almost in a begging tone. 'In that spirit you'll never see anything. Watch and learn – for your own sake, please?'

Only slightly chastened I settled to observe.

The moment he approached her she sighed and closed her eyes. The merest smile played about her lips; the rest of her lay there, utterly passive, open to receive him. What followed next I still find hard to believe. He lay upon her and moved his wand in and out of her *centre de délices* so slowly it must almost have been torture. The smile did not leave her face. She wrapped her arms and legs around him and left all the movement to him. Imperceptibly he increased his pace; he was hunting for something. Then, when he was still moving in and out no faster than the long pendulum on a clock, two seconds per swing, she moaned slightly – really just a little catch in her breath. And he settled at that. And for almost twenty minutes that is *all* he did – he moved in and out of her taking about two seconds each way.

But that was *her* rhythm. She lay there, slowly organizing her own thrill around it – knowing it would never flag, never go faster, never take her by surprise. I watched her climax gather, as on a summer's day one can watch a mighty thunderstorm massing in the distance. Yet when it came it was no storm. Her eyes might have puckered a little tighter, her lips might have fallen slightly more slack, but everything else was an enormous, contained convulsion deep in the very core of her and reaching out into every sinew.

If I had felt jealousy before, what word may I use to describe my feeling then? Just sitting there, watching her almost passive body, I knew she was experiencing something I had never yet dreamed of. All those times I believed I had been torn apart ... thought I would die ... screamed out my ecstasy – they were mere hors d'oeuvres to whatever she had just achieved.

And was still achieving! For now she was there she could stay there as long as Nero kept up that absolutely invariant rhythm. Then I had an intimation of what he meant. Here were a man and a woman whose bodies were unknown to each other an hour ago; yet they were able to go directly to this peak of pleasure. Why? It was because they shared a common language of sexual love. What other man that I had ever known (not that I had known many, of course) – what man would dream of pleasuring a woman in that common position and by means of a rhythm as invariable as a machine?

Nero, I suddenly realized, was staring into my eyes. He smiled when he saw I was coming out of my daze. I was curious to note I had lost all immediate desire for him. 'Go to bed now,' he said. 'Go to sleep. That's enough for one night.'

Monday, January 20th, 1851.
I think. The dates can be confusing because the newspapers are a few days behind here. Anyway, Nero and I are now engaged in a right royal battle of wills. I concede that he may have something to teach me – I would even say a lot – about the increase of sexual pleasure. But I do not, cannot, and will not concede that letting Bul-bull lash me with his whip has any part to play in it. That's all the difference there is between us. If he will admit that (and why not, since it is a self-evident truth?) then we can begin.

Meanwhile the other parts of my life develop in remarkable ways. He has asked me to teach the monkeys English; I have agreed, if they will teach me Arabic in return. And now Sulayah has asked to take part as well. Her one passion in life is carpet making. Like Penelope she sits at her loom and weaves away every spare moment of her husband's absence; unlike Penelope she does not pick it apart at night. But the labour proceeds as slowly, for I never saw a carpet made of such fine stitches, all of silk thread and almost too thin to be seen by the naked eye. Forty-six stitches to the inch, I counted.

Salome shows an amazing skill, which almost frightens me. She can put her hand on a part of the design and tell you its colour. I felt convinced she must have some residual sight and has been deceiving us all this while; but no – I blindfolded her and it made no difference, and even when she put her hand into a black bag containing a piece of cloth unknown to any of us (because put there by a slave outside the room), she can still do it! So it does not even rely on light at all. Yet she must touch the colour. Even three or four millimetres away and the power is lost. She says she knows Nero Bey's body in that way, too.

During the day, when I am not teaching the others or learning from them, I may read, write this diary, or go into the town – heavily guarded and wearing the full veil, of course; but I have not tried that yet.

To get back to Sulayah and her weaving. Nero asked her to lay it aside this week and take up her brush and colours to make some designs for his factory. Of course it is nowhere near ready to begin production yet, and won't be until May or even June, but he needs the designs now. She has already done some of the most mouth-watering patterns I ever saw, and is, I think, the happiest among us.

Did my early experiences with Carlos and the Duke and the encouragement from my grandmother's letters all conspire to lead me astray? Is not a richer life possible perhaps without any sexual element at all? What heresy is this! And that I should come to a *harem,* of all places, to glimpse its possibility! Or is it just my body's sour grapes?

And what of our little harem *as* a harem? The pattern was pretty much set by that first night of Nero's return. He sits amiably with us for hours after our supper, and no one even mentions the fact that he had a strangely adorable bit of gristle between his thighs where we all have an aching emptiness and that such a startling difference might lead to the most exciting possibilities. Good heavens, no!

Then he departs, and we hasten into our night attire, which does as much to shield our modesty as the plucking-out of our pubic hairs; and then we pretend to sleep. And after a while that gleaming rod of ebony comes nosing silently into our quarters, pretending to make a choice. I look up and see it, all hard and hot and glistening, waving in the air above me (and oh, he parades it for me alone, I know that) and though I know what his purpose is, I still melt and feel sick with my thwarted desire. He rules me with a rod of ebony! Indeed, so he rules us all.

And then he taps his bare foot on either one or other of the little monkeys, and sometimes they go to him one at a time, and sometimes both together. And he has as many ways of pleasing them, without ever damaging their veils of maidenhead, as he has with any other women. And they, poor sweet things, are as hopelessly in thrall to that marvellous body as every other female in this whole palace. I have not yet seen him do the same things to them twice; but with his tongue, his lips, his fingertips, his mighty hands he has a thousand ways to lift them to a frenzy of delight and keep them there till they cry mercy.

And I must sit close by them and watch it all until he asks me if I have changed my mind.

And my cry of 'Never,' sounds evermore tired every time I utter it. Yet I am nonetheless resolute,

And then the sweet, shy, young Tunisian slave girl, little Rosa, as her name translates – who now awaits his pleasure, and hers, in the harem corridor each night – comes naked into him, trembling with a desire no familiarity seems to dim; and between them they teach me what my stubbornness has cost. And yet – strangest of all – the more I learn from them, the more determined I am that he *shall* compromise with me on that one thing. The body that must

107

accept Bulbull's whip at Nero's command can never love Nero as little Rosa does. And if I stay here a whole celibate year, I will not vary that.

They have not once repeated what they did that first night – indeed, as with the little monkeys, no two nights with them are the same. He is cruel in that he knows which positions will make me ache the most for him. He remembers, I'm sure, how I cried out my ecstasy in Paris when he put me on all fours and knelt between my knees and entered me from behind ... how he gripped my buttocks in those great, gentle hands, and how he withdrew to the very tip of his knob before thrusting into me again, full and hard and like a jolt of lightning. That is precisely how he enjoyed little Rosa last night.

I believe her *fantaisie* had never stretched to it, either, for it is the only time I have seen her joy overcome her training and burst out all over her face. Her lips parted, her eyes went wide, and she sang out, 'Oh!' again and again as he knelt behind her, grinning like a demon, and thrusting away without pause. I never heard so many ways of crying, 'Oh!', each one of which turned a knife in my heart.

I have gone through so many different selves this week – hurt, indifferent, penitent, jealous, aloof, angry ... numb. But just last night I thought I detected the beginning of something new. They were lying on their sides, she curled up with her back into him; he moving slowly in and out of her from behind – and again working on her breasts and *bouton de plaisir* simultaneously. Once more she thrilled in that deep, interior way of hers, so profoundly serene and placid – and yet, in some curious way, I was no longer apart from them, watching her. I *became* her. Every voluptuous fibre in my body experienced that unknown climax, too.

Religious people, who go out into the deserts and starve their bodies of food and sensation, experience the most powerful visions and internal sensations. Has my own sexual starvation, which, in this land of plenty, is more cruel by far than theirs, produced the same kind of 'vision'? All I know is that I returned to my own chaste bed with that feeling of deep, interior peace which I have only previously experienced after enjoying the most satisfying *plaisirs*.

I am putting all this in here, Nero Bey, because, after our conversation this evening, I know you will be reading my diary from now on. You realize, I hope, that already it is you who have yielded? You say we do not discuss such matters in the harem. So when I pointed out that this rule meant we could never discuss such things at all – since even if you and I go alone into the desert, the harem – the abstract institution, which all your wonderful rules are designed to defend – *that* harem goes with us, too! Anyway, I said (I know you already know this, but I want it on record), I sit in my room in the harem and write down all my thoughts and feelings as honestly as I can. I said, 'Even if you can't face me and address these issues openly, you could at least read about what's going on inside me and find one of your own quaint ways of letting me know your side of it.' And when you agreed to *that*, Nero dear, you took one small step toward me!

Friday, Jan 31st, 1850.
Nero had to go away for a couple of days. Rosa went back to the slave quarters. If she is with child, she'll be freed – giving Nero more merit in the eyes of Allah – and become a concubine (but not one worth five swans!) and live in the harem with us.

With this interruption in our routine, I decided it was time to go on the offensive. The two little monkeys think about their sexuality all the time. When they first knew Nero Bey I suppose it was like a new toy to them, but now – and especially with Sherry, the younger one – it has turned into an unquenchable addiction that rules their lives. Any night when Nero does not relieve them, they go at each other quite desperately. But why, I thought, should it be only at night?

Sulayah was busy in her studio, painting her amazing designs, lost to the world. The two little monkeys, to whom I was supposed to be teaching English, began asking me all the words to do with sex – our sexual organs, the things they can get up to, and the thrills they give us. In talking of the things they can get up to, I told them (and this story is quite true) that Gwendolen Archer, who was our vicar's daughter, and I had once found ourselves alone in our part of the house for the whole afternoon; and so we had taken off our clothes and got into bed – different beds in different rooms – and we had a competition to see how many climaxes we could have, bringing them on with our fingers. I was twelve and she thirteen and we had each discovered those joys quite independently. When my tally reached thirty I ran giggling along the corridor and told her with great pride. She'd only managed twenty-four by then. Twenty minutes later she came scampering along to my room and burst in to tell me she'd reached forty. I'd only had seven more in that time ... and so it went on between us all afternoon until we could manage no more. And then we put on our clothes and went down and helped her mama serve tea to the Ladies' Guild for the Suppression of Vice. How they would have dropped their cakes and scalded their laps if they had known where those pale and innocent-looking young fingers had spent most of the past few hours!

Naturally the two little monkeys wanted to know what our final tally was. I have honestly forgotten. I know it was less than a hundred. I said it was a secret I had promised Gwendolen never to reveal – but, if they could surpass it, I would at least tell them that. Then they spent the whole afternoon dashing between their room and mine, their little flushed faces telling me – in English, I am proud to record! – what pleasure they were at, and their piping trebles announcing the tally. They passed a century each in ninety minutes. At 120 for Salome and 142 for Sherry, I told them they had beaten me long ago. They wore their exhaustion like a badge.

And that, Nero my darling, is why they gazed so longingly at their warm mattress when you kicked them awake for your usage tonight, and why they were so lacklustre in the Room of Joys!

Saturday, February 1st, 1851.
The day sobriety came among us. Poor young Rosa, with her master away and her eager little civet aching for exercise, I suppose, was caught in bed with another slave, a male. The penalty was a lashing of a particularly brutal kind; I cannot understand how a civilized and cultivated man like Nero Bey can permit such barbarisms under his roof and in the service of his honour. He may claim his people would misunderstand any show of clemency and that his honour is theirs and if he does not defend it, they feel defiled ... and so forth. I'm sure our own barbarous forefathers said exactly the same sort of nonsense in Europe once, but we learned better; and where we have led, why cannot others follow?

The two wretched prisoners were brought out into the courtyard, where all the floggings take place. It was a miserably cold day, which I hope dulled their feeling. The man, a tall blackamoor from Nigèr was brought out first and tied, standing up, with his feet and arms wide apart – in fact, in a copy of that letter X in which I was plucked. Only here was no frame. Just two poles in the ground, between which he was spreadeagled.

Then poor young Rosa ... the tears flow down my face as I write of it.

No, I cannot. I shall return to it tomorrow.

Nero did not come to the harem at all tonight; couldn't look me in the face, I hope.

Sunday, 2nd.
Let me try again. I got no rest at all last night. I have to write it down or it will plague me forever.

They brought out young Rosa and tied her to him, face to face, both naked. I thought it cruel enough but I did not realize its especial cruelty. Then everyone waited for a signal from the Bey. We were all forced to sit on the harem balcony, nearby. The two wretches were not twelve feet away. I could see every shiver of their flesh, every goosepimple. Rosa turned and stared directly at Nero Bey; I never saw such pleading in any mortal eyes before.

And what was going on in his mind? Did he then remember the hours and hours of joy he had craved of that flesh, courteously asking its permission, first? What did all that gentleness and tenderness between them add up to at that moment? How when the Day of Judgement comes can he look his merciful Allah in the face and say, 'I took all that pleasure from the body of that sweet young girl and gave her all that agony in return?'

Their eyes were locked for a long moment – so long I thought he would at last show a mercy greater than his pride. Now, who can say? Perhaps it was only to prolong her agony. Anyway, he gave Bulbull the signal – a wave of his hand, as cool as a breeze. And then the eunuch started to ply his lash, which he did without pity.

It was not the so-called 'soft' whip he keeps for the harem women but a thick, stiff pole of leather, about six feet long, with whippy hide at its end, burnished to a fierce gleam. With this he can deliver cuts of enormous power and accuracy, making only the merest flick of those huge, sleek, powerful arms. He loved that work so much, I think our eyes were fixed more on him than on his wretched victims. With every flick he brought forth a roar or a scream from one or other of them. The man he cut to ribbons, but Rosa he 'merely' painted all over in bright scarlet weals. Then the inevitable happened.

The man, carried beyond all self-control by so much pain, had an erection. I watched aghast as that pink-brown knob came nosing up between her open thighs. Bulbull was waiting for it, too, for he let it grow hard and stiff. How he must have hated the sight of that urgent organ! He above all, who was made impotent by the surgeon's knife, who wielded an ultimate power – short of actual life and death – over those two trussed and helpless creatures, was yet mocked by one of them, and in the one way that most directly taunted his impotence. He drew back his lash and gave it the most vicious cut of all. The man passed mercifully out of consciousness.

I turned to Nero Bey. I never saw a man so black to turn so pale. And I murmured softly for his ear alone, 'If he gives either of them one stroke more, I shall leave this place tonight and never return.'

I think he was about to give the signal to stop in any case, but that is not the way it appeared to Bulbull. Turning to his master with a grin of triumph, he saw the hateful foreign she-devil whispering in the man's ear. And next minute the master cries stop. Now, if ever he were allowed near me with his whip – even the 'soft' one he keeps for us females – he would slice me in two with it, I'm sure.

Again Nero Bey did not come to our harem tonight, but Sulayah began asking me questions about our notorious floggings in the British army. So that is your response to my little lecture on barbarism, my dear! My answer is that I'm sure all the finest elements in our civilization heartily wish the practice were ended; only those vicious, hidebound generals with brains the size of peas oppose it. And the question for you, my darling, is which side you would prefer to count yourself among?

Why do I call you darling after such a display? That was quite unthinking. I never wanted so desperately to hold you in my arms as I do tonight – not only for our sexual pleasure but to show you what love and tenderness can do. There is a gentle man in you, at war with your people's ancient barbarism. Find some way to show me he is not dead, I beg you. I love him so much.

February 3rd.
The two monkeys have changed, and this time it had nothing to do with me. I thought the lashing of the two miscreants had left them singularly unaffected – possibly because they could not see the worst of it. But they now approach our Master with such a different mien. Their 'modest reluctance' has become genuine and he draws out their lust with the greatest difficulty.

I believe they now understand that my 'battle' with Nero Bey is, in a strange way, theirs, too. It is the battle of all women in all harems with their Lord and Master. Perhaps it is the battle of all females with all men everywhere. Men love us, adore us, cannot make too many trips to our wells. And so they devise an infinity of cunning ways to prevent other men from making that same journey. The first is love itself – which should be all that is needed between true and equal partners. The second is the addiction they plant in us along with their seed – that overpowering desire for the feel of their stiff, hard organs filling our oracles and spreading the joy of it in tumultuous spending throughout our bodies. That addiction we can tolerate if there be love to shield it.

But now, when the Rod of Ebony that rules us all here comes nosing and questing through the harem, what do we see as the true origin of its power here? His love for us? Our almost unbearable longing to feel that sweetest flesh in all the world between our thighs? No! Take them away and our world is still not empty – for there at last, revealed for all to see, is the true source of his power over us: Bulbull and his whips.

This is no fanciful elaboration of an event too painful otherwise to bear. We women actually lived through that moment of revelation when Nero hesitated before giving his signal to the eunuch. His oft-murmured declarations of love in Rosa's ear had failed. Her addiction to his wand had failed. Did he then say to himself, 'These are my two legitimate means of binding this woman to me. They have failed. So be it. I am not God. I cannot win every venture. Let her now stay with her new lover ...'? No. He gave the signal that said, 'All else has been stripped away. Now let my women see my true power

– undisguised by talk of love, by smiles, by gentle caresses, by any of those pleasures with which I *pretend* to sustain it. Lash away, good Bulbull! Bind these women to me in their very blood!'

And that, Nero Bey, is why Salome and Sherry are no longer those two girlish hedonists of old. You had taught them that sexual delight was all that bound you and them together; and for them it would, I think, have held for life. But last week you showed them how wickedly you had deceived them all this while. For now, when they take your big hard *antenne* in their nimble little fingers, they feel it taper off into a couple of feet of cruelly burnished hide. *You* may not see it; but *we* know it is there.

You should go back to pleasuring with Sulayah; she adores you for what you did, sees nothing wrong in flogging your failures to death, and would gladly accept the Six Marks of Submission every day if you but asked it.

Feb 9th.

A new tactic. Now Sulayah brings him a different girl up from the slave quarters each night and the monkeys and I must stand and watch. Those gentle, yielding girls and women are all very excited to be chosen to please the Bey and do their utmost to gratify him in every way. But he cannot hide that desperation in his eye. Something tells him he is losing this battle and he cannot see how. The girls moan and shiver with their ecstasy at the magic working of his ebony wand inside them; and that loving weapon stays hot and stiff as ever, through many bouts – more, not fewer, as his desperation grows. But down there in the slave quarters lies his conqueror, bruised and hurting. Her pain wounds us all. And while he refuses to accept that, she will win.

116

What next? This evening he asked me to take Rosa into my room and nurse her back to health. Until she is well again, I may sleep in there with her and need not watch his rutting with the slaves. I asked him what of the man, Rosa's lover. He mumbled that the fellow is in hospital and a surgeon from Tunis has treated him and he will not lose his penis after all.

What an effect this change has wrought! Just as I had sung poor Rosa to sleep, Salome came running to me in great excitement with her mouth wide open. She wanted to show me it was full of Nero's semen. He had never before done that to her, but he took her to the Room of Joys tonight and asked her what she wished them to do – and that was her choice. Sherry, she said, was now repeating the nice new trick with him and it wasn't fair; she'd had to wait until she was considered old enough, so why should the younger one be given the privilege straight away?

I did not tell her so, but I suppose Nero was desperate for some show of affection that did not depend on the lash.

Now he has left us for a week. I think Rosa's bruises will be almost mended again by the time he returns. What is to become of her then? Not a word has been said.

Feb 23rd.
Nero Bey has brought a new concubine! A lovelier creature I think never breathed. She is nineteen years old. Her mother was Chinese, her father an Ethiop, and the mixture of those two kinds of beauty far transcends either. She has a comeliness that takes one's breath away. Sulayah and I gasped when we saw her. Her name is Ouné, and she is both beautiful and voluptuous.

While she was being prepared to accept the Six Marks of Submission – which she assented to without the slightest demur –

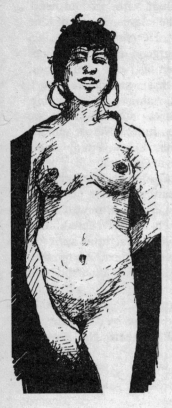

I examined her naked body as minutely as possible, seeking some slight flaw; and there was none. Her proportions are perfect; her breasts round and firm with lovely large nipples; her belly almost concave and soft; her *derrière* pert and solid; her hairless mound is curved and delicately shaded, with its cleft crisp and firmly drawn. Her skin is of a deep honey colour, almost like amber, and her hair jet black. Her cheekbones are large and exquisite; her eyes are heavy-lidded, dark, remote, and dreamy. Her nose is slightly retroussé and her finely arched nostrils reveal a woman of subtlety and taste. Her lips are full and sensuous; and even another woman, I think, would want to kiss them.

But this catalogue of parts can in no way convey the overwhelming impression of sensuality that hangs about her like an aura. Just to look at her is to feel oneself overcome by a warm, dark, spicy sort of languor. She radiates a sexual compulsion that I think no man could resist. Nero is completely in thrall to her already.

When she was well stretched between the gilded frame, Sulayah and two slaves hauled it into the upright position. Then Bulbull stepped forward, swinging his 'soft' whip through the air and making the most ferocious, gun-like cracks with it in the air. But the lashes he gave her deceived no one. Six moderately hard slaps with a bare hand would have hurt her more; no wonder she did not even gasp, much less cry out. And the look of reproach you gave me, Nero Bey, for refusing something so mild! Well, we both know it would be quite different if your eunuch ever had *me* stretched before him in that frame. Besides, that is not the point. The whip itself must go. It is the symbol that leads you astray in assessing your power over us.

When it was done, Nero untied her himself and led her at once to the Room of Joys. There, while Sulayah and I watched from outside and the two monkeys listened, he explored her every charm — with his eyes, with his lips, his fingers, his hands, his tongue. And all the time she just stood or sat, knelt or lay, with her gaze averted and a purring sort of smile on her lips. Her cranny was so wet by the time he finished that he needed only to press the knob of his wand anywhere between her thighs in order to enter her heavenly portals.

Then he began what I can only describe as a kind of sexual ballet between them. He bent her forward over a chair and slowly entered her from behind, taking about five seconds to complete the stroke — and the same amount of time to withdraw, pulling her upright at the same time. Then in again in that upright position, with the same intense deliberation — and out. On each outward stroke he gently handled her into a new position: sideways to him with one foot on the chair; face to face; then, still standing, with one thigh thrown around him; then both. Then he sat on the chair and pulled her onto him, with her back to him; again with her sideways on; then with her thighs straddling him, face to face.

In each position, while that thick, passionate rapier of his was stirring her cauldron, his hands, his fingers, his tongue were working at the rest of her like fluttering birds. From the moment he touched her she was carried aloft in wave after wave of voluptuousness, dark, sultry, and heavy. They finished their *pas de deux* on a pile of silken pillows, where her ecstasy was like a deep, glowing lake of passion that rose and drowned him.

I woke in the small hours, remembered it, and wept. She heard me and came into my bed and took me in her arms and hummed a song into my ears that calmed me wonderfully. Her body smelled of him and I was comforted.

This morning two palace carpenters came to the antechamber to the harem, where Ouné was at once conducted by Sulayah. They applied all sorts of curious instruments to her, jointed structures of wood, which they adjusted and then clamped with butterfly screws. What can it mean?

It is now two months since any man's *chandelle* has stretched my *puits de Vénus*; during that time I have been forced to stand – or sit, or lie – and watch one of the most superb male organs in all the world at work on – nay, *in* – bodies far less deserving than mine; little *ignorantes* who know nothing of the power and majesty of a true climax ... slave girls who would be happy enough if he never stuck anything more potent than his finger inside them. How can he leave me like this? How can you do it, Nero? Has your own body no memories to mourn?

Do you not remember that night we spent together in Paris? The unparallelled joys we found in each other's bodies? Don't tell me such experiences were commonplace to you. Not one of these girls can get you going more than twice. You spent eight times with me, in my womb, in my mouth. Your life has not been so rich in such experiences that you can afford to let me languish unused much longer. You'll see. Not even Ouné will satisfy you as I could – if only you would drop your stiff-necked demand that Bulbull be allowed to butcher me first.

Ouné is an extraordinary young girl. Is she human at all, I wonder? I don't think you realize what she's doing to you, Nero Bey. When she lies there beneath you, every silken muscle in her body so totally relaxed and submissive to you – with her eyes downcast and with that enigmatic little half-smile on her lips ... when she begins to give out those little moans of happiness, which grow in a crescendo of gasps and sighs ... those little whimpering noises in her throat – and finally those sibilant whisperings of *yes!* and *oh please!* – do you know what it does to you? I stand outside the Room of Joys, watching you, and I see an increasing desperation in your eyes. You become possessed by an urge to please her more ... and more ... and yet more. Your own pleasure has dwindled away to that one over-riding compulsion – to give her just one thrill more.

As a cuckoo hatchling is able to drive its adoptive parents to distraction with its incessant demands for food, so Ouné will soon reduce you to a chattering, ravelled skeleton with her incessant demands for *Plaisir* and yet more *Plaisir*. Hers is not a thrill-*giving* cleft, like mine (which is what any young concubine's ought to be, in my view), she herself – her whole voluptuous, passive body – is a dedicated thrill-*demanding* machine, a moloch that will absorb all the life-juice you can feed it and will then go on to devour your organ, your desire, your life itself ...

The monkeys were at their plucking again today – a service they perform for us every week. Now, of course, it is nowhere near so painful as that first marathon session. Ouné says she was plucked from the moment she began to grow those hairs. I asked her when she lost her virginity (she speaks French as well as Arabic) and she laughed and said only a week before the Bey bought her. Our town, Sidi-el-Barrès, is apparently a brothel town, where the French soldiers are sent for their recreation. There are over forty brothels in all and she had been destined for the one that is reserved for senior officers.

'You're much better off here,' I commented.

'I don't know,' she sighed. 'There is something pleasurable in the thought of four or five different men breaking their desire upon me every night.'

There is a tribe in the mountains, she says, the Tauneg, who send their young girls down into those houses to earn their dowries. And they think it no shame to take pleasure of all their customers. The Arab girls despise them for their uninhibited ways; but the Frenchmen, of course, love them for the same reason. And they go back very rich – and not too long in harness for their bodies to be spoiled by the heavy traffic they endure with so many ardent men to pursue them.

She tells me all this with a note of wistful regret.

So, Nero Bey, if you wish to keep your latest concubine satisfied, send for the rhino horn, the goat's testicles, the Spanish fly, and all your other remedies for failing potency!

Incidentally, one can now see the wisdom of Nero Bey in siting his factory here – apart from the fact that it is his own town. There is a steady supply of unsuitable or used-up young girls with nimble fingers in the weeding out of all those houses.

Sherry came quietly to me, shortly after they had finished their plucking and asked whether I had realized that Ouné's body and mine are identical in size, shape, and proportion; only her nipples are larger than mine. I had not noticed it, I must say. The difference in our colouring and faces is great, and that perhaps misled me. I must make a comparison next chance I get.

Tuesday, March 25th.
Today we have the explanation for that strange activity with the carpenters and Ouné. An elaborate contraption made in costly inlaid wood and upholstered here and there in deeply buttoned velvet was this morning brought into the Room of Joys. Sulayah at once took Ouné in there and made her take off all her clothes. The two monkeys ran in to discover what the excitement was.

The contraption is a special kind of bed – a Couch of Venus, one could call it – of a most ingenious kind, exactly made to Ouné's measurements. When she lies face down upon it, the broad, padded spine supports her from her mound to her head; there are two scooped out hollows where her breasts may hang and a hole in either side, level with her navel, where Nero Bey may insert his hand and get his fingers at her rosebud. Thus she can lie in full, voluptuous ease and be enjoyed in the 'doggy' position – which is otherwise quite strenuous for a slim young girl with a vigorous and passionate lover like Nero.

And it was the same with all the other strenuous positions – flat on the back, knees bent, thighs apart, and *concon* angled up, begging to be stretched; the Couch of Venus supports her pelvis and limbs in the perfect position from Nero's point of view.

Another angle allows her to sit half up, spreading herself for the gratification of his lips and tongue; and here the supports for his arms let his hands fall naturally and easily on her breasts.

Another allows her to lie on her side, bent at her hips with her thighs raised for him to penetrate her from behind; tunnels beneath the padded shelf on which she lies permit his hands to explore her front without the weight of her body falling on his arm – which is usually what makes men abandon that delicious position before the girl has enjoyed its possibilities to the full.

In short, this amazing new couch will allow Ouné and Nero to enjoy all those strenuous positions where joy is usually curtailed by the cramping and tiring of their muscles. Watching her try out each new position, I thought, *If only I had the Duke's stereoscopic camera here, what pictures I could give Nero Bey of his voluptuous young concubine, positioned and spread so perfectly for his delight!*

March 26th.
They tried it out last night – every possible position. The most amazing of all was the 'doggy' one, which encourages her to arch her back into an almost unbelievable curve, thrusting her pert young *derrière* up in an attitude that almost screams *please!* Nero has tried that position with her before, usually on his long stool, which flattens her breasts and leaves only the edges of her nipples available for his stimulation

– she being too drugged by her own sexual pleasure to raise her body and admit his hands there. But now she can sink into that semi-coma of hers while he can now go on and on, filling her with thrill after thrill. Oh, Nero Bey, who is the slave now?

In our endless battle of penis *vs* vagina, can it be that the utterly passive young concubine, who does nothing except lie still in whatever position you choose, and who sinks at once into a stupor of bliss ... has she discovered the secret that has eluded me all this time? Can the meek and passive vagina, after all, subdue the mighty rod of ebony and allow us to thumb our noses at the lash that backs its power?

My thoughts turn to Bulbull.

Friday, April 18th.
I must now tell the astonishing story of the past two weeks ... is it only two weeks? I was unable to write a word, since I knew Nero Bey reads everything sooner or later.

My hint about the camera was taken up in the strangest way. Nero Bey came to me and said Sulayah could only do her designs at a certain scale – about a third of the actual carpet. If she tried to work at the full scale, everything went flat and dull. The line lost its verve; the areas of colour failed to harmonize one with another. Would it be possible for me to take photographs of her one-third-scale designs and enlarge them to full size for the jacquard pattern makers to work from? Colour was unnecessary, since they could always refer to the third-scale original.

'With the strength of this sun, nothing would be easier,' I said. 'If only I had a camera.'

Well! Equipment that would set the mouths watering among the finest photographers in Paris was delivered the following morning! In two days, all her so-far-completed designs were available in black-and-white enlargements, on paper and at full scale, in the jacquard-design studio. I was excused all nightly harem duties during this time, which, in my case, of course, involved watching Nero and Ouné – and the two monkeys for hors d'oeuvres – at their pleasure ... which, I may admit it now, nearly broke my heart.

I have been deliberately withholding all expression of my hurt in this diary, so that he should not be able to gloat and feel he had brought me near to breaking – which, indeed, he had. What he did not know was that when I break, it is not in the places, nor in the directions, he might desire.

The last straw came when he asked me to take some stereos of him at his *exercises d'amour* with his two little slaves and his one functioning concubine. This involved a severe break with tradition, for we all had to go out on the roof garden and use the sun for our light. We tried both limelight and an electrical arc but in the confined space of the Room of Joys it just made everyone cough and sneeze and it looked like an orgy of hay-fever victims.

Once he had the stereos, the number of nights on which he came nosing through the harem with that ebony weapon throbbing away in front of him, diminished. He was often 'away on palace business' or 'working for the Dey' or simply 'something to do with the new factory.'

On these occasions Ouné slips into my bed and we talk and dream about the future, endlessly. My ownership of the Vallodon girls intrigues her. When my year is up, she wants me to take her with me to Paris, where she thinks we could set up in business as the very topmost cream of my own *crème de la crème!* 'I could baiser the men,' she says, 'and you could sell them photographs of them and me together.'

126

We tried pleasuring each other, for, in my desperation I think I would have tried a dog; but it was no use. She behaved with me as she does with Nero – she just lay there and accepted all the thrills my fingers, my thigh, and my tongue could give her! Our only possible position was labia-to-labia, which, though stimulating, is monotonous after a while – and not a very long while, either.

Then, when the Bey came back from one of his mysterious absences, he suddenly issued orders that I was on no account to watch himself and Ouné at their *exercises*. What was in his mind, I wonder? Was he fed up with my constant observation that Ouné's passivity had enslaved his vigour? Did he imagine that my mind's eye would embroider memory with scenes of fantastical joy that would finally break me? Well, he would have been right there – but for one small circumstance.

Sulayah was often in her studio until late at night. (Strange how our rigid harem rules may always be set aside for commerce! When humanity knocks at that same door – rules became rules again.) So my only trustworthy gaoler was Bulbull.

So that I would be sure to hear Ouné's little gasps and moans of rapture, I was to kneel at Bulbull's feet against the north wall of the Room of Joys – the one opposite the ladies' quarters – where he normally slept. I was to have my back facing the pierced brickwork so that I could not see. This meant Bulbull had to face me, to make sure of his charge. And that, in turn, meant that he was almost forced to watch his master and his concubine, or the slave of the night, at their dalliance.

After about half an hour on that first evening I began to get a cramp in my knee. I half rose to ease it and was immediately pushed down by that vile creature whom I could not call man. But then, instead of taking his hand away, he left it on my head, resting delicately ... almost tenderly.

And there was no doubting his tenderness when, a moment later, he began to stroke my hair in gentle circles. If that was not startling enough, the bulge that began to swell his pantaloons almost knocked me over – literally, too, for it was no shrivelled little swelling. It was not a full erection, of course, but it was the beginnings of something very interesting.

I was in a turmoil of thought at this. Had he been cheating Nero Bey all these years? I always thought they were docked 'smack-smooth,' as horsey people say: no penis, no testicles, no scrotum – just a little puckered hole for their urine to escape. Seeing that it was not so – at least not in Bulbull's case – a desperate plan began to form almost at once. Indeed, it was fully formed the moment I remembered the details of M Vallodon's ecstatic death.

Without any preliminary I opened my lips and took that half-hard bulge into my mouth, sucking vigorously and making him as wet as possible. He gasped, accepted it for a moment, and then thrust me rudely away. The soft lump fell away almost at once. But I had felt two surges of blood in that time – and that was all I needed to know. From then on there was about two feet between us and I did not stir until the couple in the Room of Joys had finished their pleasures.

Next day I went to Bulbull and said, 'Bulbull, we've lived under the same roof for some months, now. Don't you think it's time we tried to come to some sort of understanding?'

He grinned. 'I can do nothing, great and gracious lady, until you accept the Six Marks of Submission.'

'If I do,' I asked, 'will you be gentle with me?'

'I will apply the law,' he responded stiffly.

'Yes, of course you must. I see that. But will you apply it as gently as you did with Ouné?'

I could see his dilemma in every wrinkle on his brow. If he said yes, his honour would force him to keep his word; if he said no, then I might persist in my refusal. And he desperately wanted to see the colour of my blood. That was all I wanted to know. But his hesitation served my other purpose, which was to back him into some trap like this, where he had to make some reply and yet dared not be honest, and then offer him a second topic as a way out – apparently forgetting my first question. So I asked him if he had ever enjoyed a girl, before …

'In my youth …' he began and then shook his head. 'It's no business of yours.'

'Of course not,' I assured him. Then I grinned. 'D'you know why Nero Bey asked me to come here as his concubine?'

'That,' he replied haughtily, 'I'll never understand.'

'Then you don't know the story! Do you know, for instance, he's paying me more money simply to be here than he spent in building this entire palace?'

His lips curled in a sneer of derision. 'It's true,' I assured him. 'Ask him yourself. Anyway, the reason is …' And I went on to tell him a slightly coloured version of the Vallodon story.

The sneer was less in evidence when he turned on his heel and left; indeed, I thought he looked decidedly pensive.

That night he was again my invigilator. I perfumed my hair for the first time in weeks and I bathed and oiled my body as if Nero himself had yielded. Poor Bulbull could not help himself. The moment Ouné began her gentle, hour-long crescendo, the eunuch began to caress my hair – and moments later the

129

folds of his pantaloons were being thrust out toward me. Again it was not a full erection, but it was more than Vallodon had given me to work on.

I had tried all day to get elastic bands but it seemed that a mighty palace could function perfectly without them. For the moment I would have to use my fingers – rather as a milkmaid milks a cow, only in this case 'milking' the blood toward the knob and squeezing it there. And for that I needed to get my hand above him, putting the tip of my thumb against the top of his organ at its root and using my four nimble fingers to squeeze the sensitive underside, in sequence, against my palm and thumb.

I pulled apart the folds of his pantaloons and there it came nosing out, half flaccid and pointing downward at about forty-five degrees. I raised my elbow as high as possible to get my hand into the right relationship. It was agonizing but I managed to stiffen him up in just over half a dozen pulls. This was much better than I thought, for the more easily a man has an erection without their help, the more lethal the rubber bands will prove.

I was astonished then at the size of his organ. It wasn't particularly long but it was about as thick as a girl would wish to let inside her – and I now desperately wished to get this one inside me, rubber bands and all.

He gasped at what I had done. Before he could stop me I took it all into my mouth and, nearly choking at every movement, got it as deep into my throat as I could manage. But it did not last. Without the magic of the elastic bands, his stiffness left him and he was soft again.

'That always happens,' he whispered mournfully.

'I can stop it,' I assured him. 'If you will let me try the trick I used with M Vallodon?'

He stared at me in alarm.

I smiled. 'Can I stand up and whisper in your ear?'

He stared at Nero Bey as if he thought we were visible from in there – or as if the two on the Couch of Venus, the one lost in her deep, dark pools of ecstasy, the other going desperate to fill them, would take the slightest interest in us. 'Please?' I added.

He took away his hand. 'Very well, then.'

I stood and, pressing my body ardently against him, whispered, 'I can control it now. I learned that since. Also he was an old man of eighty, broken down by years of debauchery. You are a strong and vigorous young man. It could not possibly do you any harm.'

He put an arm around me and began to caress my body through its thin gauzy covering. Having not felt the touch of a man for nearly four months, I'm ashamed to say I found it an incredibly erotic experience, even though I loathed the man. My grandmother once wrote to me of the unbelievable joy of being rogered (her word) by a man you loathe; I did not believe her until then.

The thing was, he made me feel feminine again. I became aware of all those feminine things about me – the curve of my hips, the softness of my skin, the arch of my back, the desireable swelling of my *derrière*, the ripe fullness of my breasts, the delicate poise of my neck, my perfume ... and above all, my longing to feel the *joujou* of even that odious person go nosing up into the aching void of my *centre de plaisirs* ... is that not the most feminine sensation of all? He awoke it all in me and I found myself covering his face and lips with kisses and assuring him that I hoped I would never yield to Nero Bey for he, Bulbull, was all a young girl could desire in a man. God help me but at the time I said it I'm not sure I didn't actually mean it!

Next day I stained some photographic prints with potassium permanganate and told Nero that the air was getting into some of the chemicals and making them discolour. What I needed was a few good elastic bands to hold down some oilcloth around the necks of the bottles. He sent out a slave who brought me much too many – for that purpose.

But that night there was no cavorting in the Room of Joys, nor the next two, either; Bulbull had to contain his excitement and wait three whole days. But, oh, it was worth it. He was absolutely trembling with desire by the time we were together again, and his pego was almost fully erect without any help from me – beyond the fact of my existence and the perfumes that rose from my scantily clad body.

In fact, the first thing I did was take everything off – both him and me. They really had done the smallest job imaginable on him; even the sac of his scrotum was intact, along with all those sensitive nerves – and no over-sensitive testicles to turn pleasure into pain. I had intended placing the rubber bands (in the manner I must not reveal) and then sucking him to maximum stiffness before letting him into me; but he was so stiff already by the time I applied the bands that I just lay down and pulled him on top of me. He was huge – as big as Bearski that night at Vallodon's. And I'm sorry to have to place it on record, but he was every bit as enjoyable, too.

I dared not cry out, of course, nor make any sound above the merest whisper. I just lay there, living again through the indescribable delight of a climax from deep within my well of paradise – and waiting for him to die of an apoplexy.

Which was the one thing he steadfastly refused to do. The beast actually came inside me! No juices, of course, but I could feel that great thing throbbing away inside me, stirring me to even greater ecstasy.

Nero was exhausted earlier than usual that night. Bulbull and I only just got dressed in time. Now indeed I was in a quandary. I had been paid one of the highest sums in history (surely?) to be a concubine for a year in the harem of a black adonis, and instead was to spend the time being relieved by his eunuch – a creature of loathing to me!

I went out to be alone on the palace roof garden, saying I had some contact frames to expose. Bulbull, who had been watching me like a hawk all morning, followed me out. There was no need for him to be circumspect, of course; he was expected to keep an eye on all the females and could get as close as he liked to any of them without arousing any suspicion other than that he was working zealously on his master's behalf.

He came and stood beside me. 'If you will now accept the Six Marks of Submission,' he murmured, 'I will be even more gentle than I was with Ouné. The Bey will not mind. I would not have dared hurt you in any case. He told me he would slit my throat if I truly hurt you.'

I sighed. 'I'm afraid it makes no difference, Bulbull. Gentle or fierce, I shall never submit in that way. It is a matter of principle.'

'I agree,' he said.

I turned to him in astonishment.

'Whatever you do, great and gracious lady – it is right. You can do no wrong in my sight. I ...' He choked. Tears began to flow down his face.

I did not know what to do. I touched his bare forearm hesitantly. And he just stood there, crying.

'Bulbull?' I murmured.

'I love you,' he sobbed. Then, taking a grip on himself, he started to explain in choking words. 'What you have restored to me ... the beauty of it – you are so beautiful. I think you are a goddess come to earth ...' It just went on pouring out of him in a welter of incoherence. He was like a young boy overwhelmed by the power of love for the first time. And when he had finished, I found that the last shreds of my dislike for him had vanished. I actually longed for that evening to come, bringing with it the possibility of the renewal of our joys.

Something of my change of mood must have penetrated his consciousness for he grew calmer and eventually had himself completely in hand again.

'Tonight,' I said.

He saw I meant it and was over the moon.

Of course, the inevitable happened. We made so much noise in our ecstasy that Nero Bey came running to see what was going on. Well! I honestly thought he was going to kill us on the spot. He began shrieking like a demon, kicking at the pair of us, not caring what hurt he did.

I leaped up at once and shouted back at him: It was all my fault. I had led Bulbull astray and he was not to blame.

Nero was determined to flog him to death anyway.

I said that if he received even one lash, I would leave. He could have his money back. Who wanted it anyway? It reeked of his arrogance and pride and obstinacy. And I'd blacken his name in Paris. No one there would buy his carpets any more.

He told me he'd have me flogged to death, too.

I asked who'd photograph Sulayah's designs then? An outsider? Someone who'd sell spare prints to all his competitors?

He started literally to foam at the mouth then.

At that moment Sulayah came in, drawn by all the noise. She took one look at us, summed up the situation, and dragged the two monkeys away with her, back to the harem. Between them they manhandled the gilded frame into the Room of Joys and then came back for me. I shook their greedy hands away. 'I'll come without force,' I said. 'Do what you like to me, but I'm warning you, if Bulbull is hurt in any way, I'm going.'

'Do what I like, eh?' Nero echoed. The spittle showered from him. 'Oh, we can make you regret *that* invitation, little beauty!'

They led me to the Room of Joys, Sulayah grim and dutiful, having a real *plaisir* of dutifulness; the monkeys chattering away excitedly, not having the faintest idea why; Ouné withdrawn and pale; and Nero working himself back into a fury again. 'How dare you? How *dare* you? When I think of it! A eunuch! To get him into that disgusting condition ...'

They tied me face down, spreadeagled in that familiar letter X.

'Shall I get the whip, my lord?' Sulayah asked.

'No.' There was a smile in his voice. 'The scorpions.'

I remembered them then – the switches of light, whippy wood with which the palace slaves had cleared a path for me on the day of my arrival.

The monkeys ran off to fetch a couple; when they returned they swished them through the air, producing a fierce whistling noise. They struck at a few cushions, too – making me wince at the thought of the pain I could no longer avoid.

Sulayah and Nero grabbed at the scorpions and started to swish them above me. To my astonishment, little Sherry stood near my head and bent herself over, nearly double. 'Me first!' she begged in an excited voice.

135

Nero laughed and gave her a playful sting. She shrieked with delight and, slipping off her clothes, bent over again and said, 'More! All over my back.'

Again Nero laughed and obliged her, swishing away until she cried, 'Enough!'

By then Salome was beside her, also naked and begging for the same privilege.

It gave Nero an idea. He knelt beside me and, speaking soft and low, murmured, 'Tell me, little one, have you ever taken a pleasure to the point where it turns imperceptibly into pain?'

I said nothing; to tell the truth, I was trembling too much to trust my voice at all.

'Shall we try it with this?' He stroked my naked flesh with his scorpion. Lovingly … lingeringly. 'Don't scream out until it turns to pain,' he said.

Then, kneeling at my left, with Sulayah at my right, he began to thrash me with those same playful strokes he had used on the little girls. The extraordinary thing was that, with my fears so sharp and every nerve in my body bunched up tight against the expected torment of those scorpions, these gentle strokes *were* an astonishing kind of pleasure. My unfinished ecstasy with Bulbull came flooding back to me and took over in that rain of gentleness. The mild stinging was like a fiery glow all over me, like a hundred hot hands caressing my skin.

'The other side,' Nero said. Again I could tell his condition from his voice. He was sexually excited by this exercise; I could hear the catch in his breathing, the tremble in his tone.

They manhandled the frame over, laying me on my back. How cool the silk felt against my excited flesh. Then a new terror seized me. 'Not my breasts!' I pleaded. 'Don't hit my nipples.' They were hard already with my delight.

'You two,' Nero commanded. 'Protect them.' And he laughed when those two little monkeys sat on me – the little devils! – and began to use my nipples as firm friction posts to bring them to their ecstasy. And all the while that rain of gentle, glowing strokes from the scorpions fell on my stomach, my unprotected mound, my spreadeagled thighs.

What with those two little minxes reaching their petty thrills on my nipples, and the one man I desired more than any other in the world squatting beside me, exciting himself and me with those glowing tickles – for they really were little more than that – it was not long before I was out of control again, moaning and gasping with the sort of full-blooded ecstasy he had not heard since our night in Paris.

It was finally too much for him. He swept the little monkeys aside and threw himself flat upon me, going in at once and beginning to thrash away, in and out, like an engine gone berserk. I longed for my legs to be free, that I could throw my thighs up around him and keep him there until he spent. But all I could do was thrash and moan and grab at that magnificent ebony wand with my hips.

'Submit?' he asked in a fierce whisper.

'Yes, yes!' I cried but in such a confusion of joy it could have been the universal assent of *plaisir* itself – which is the loudest *yes!* any of us can cry to the gift of rampant manhood.

Almost too late he saw his danger. For if he spent into me now, with no true Marks of Submission upon my flesh, I would have won. I shouldn't have let that thought enter my head, for I'm sure it communicated to him – just as my earlier joy had done. He withdrew in a panic while there was still time and looked about him for another vessel in which to pour all that pent-up lust.

Ouné turned and fled. Salome lifted her eyebrows expectantly, hoping against hope. He stared longingly at me and then, having no alternative left, threw Sulayah on her back in a deep pile of cushions and thrust himself into her, apologizing for what he was forced to do and trying to get his orgasm over and done with as quickly as possible.

To his amazement – to the amazement of us all – she began at once to have a thrill of her own, then another, and another ... And there was no fight-me-for-it modesty about her, either. I doubt I myself have ever been less inhibited than Sulayah was that night; he stormed her femininity, taking it so much by surprise that her defences of false modesty (and doesn't this just show how false they are!), weakened by those long years of disuse, fell at his first thrust.

When he finally remembered to come, she let out one great moan of satisfaction – and fell sound asleep beneath him.

Ouné had meanwhile untied my bonds. 'Well tame him between us now,' she whispered as she massaged the white bands of flesh around my wrists. When Nero flopped down in exhausted surprise, she at once lay upon him and took his shrinking wand between those voluptuous lips – swiftly reversing its decline. Meanwhile I straddled him and offered his mouth my secret oyster to explore. An hour later I think he knew what exhaustion truly is.

April 29th.
All these nights we never saw him. It took him so long to accept what had happened.

Which of us has won? Neither.

Is the battle still on? Probably. It has just shifted its ground, that's all.

Tonight that superb rod of ebony, which has ruled me as an absentee landlord for so long, came thrusting and nosing among us females again, seeking a soft, warm, and complaisant *vagin* to shroud it in relief. And at last he chose me. He did not kick me as he kicks the little monkeys; nor did he lower his knob to my lips for a submissive kiss, as he does to Ouné; instead, and with a devilish grin on his face, he reached up beneath my covering, caught hold of my harem pants by their ankles, and whipped them off me in one swift pull.

I rose and walked before him into the Room of Joys, and oh what a feast I made of those few paces! If the languorous swaying of my hips did not remind him of the bliss we once had shared, if the swish of my bare thighs as they brushed together did not recall the softness of my flesh, and if the stickiness of the juice that was already flowing from me did not make him remember a *canal amoureux* he had once called pure cream – than he was dead; but I had the fiery heat of that pale-brown knob only inches from its goal to tell me he was very much alive-oh!

Those little monkeys were right about one thing: My body must be very close to Ouné's in all our essential measurements, for the Couch of Venus suited me to a T, or an X, a W, a V ... and all the other shapes I assumed for his delectation during the next hour or so. But it had the most extraordinary effect on me. I had seen her adopt those same positions so often by now – lying there, completely submissive, withdrawing herself into the bottomless well of her own sensuality, smiling loosely, and giving out those little moans and whimpers of ecstasy that forced him to go on working at their increase. All this was now so much a part of that couch, it compelled me to follow suit. And I truly do not think

I have ever enjoyed an ecstasy quite like it – a long sequence of ecstasies, flowing into and out of each other like great glowing caverns of pleasure inside.

He made a new discovery, too. How is it that not one of my previous lovers, who have surely kissed and caressed every inch of my skin, never discovered it? A little way down my spine from the base of my neck is a spot whose sensitivity I can only describe (now) as infinite. Until he discovered it I had believed I had already made every possible act of submission to him, withholding nothing. But when his lips settled there, when the wild, flickering tip of his tongue trembled on that spot, I felt every nerve and fibre and atom of me melt and dissolve. It was as if a volcano that had been waiting to erupt inside me simply melted and collapsed instead, spreading pure fire into every part of me. He felt it at once, of course, and, beautiful devil that he is, he began giving me little bites on that same place. From then on I was an utter slave to his desires.

Still giving me those little bites, he arched his back and brought his knob to the inner curtains of my love canal, gently teasing them up and down, craving an entry that had never been more craved in return. And slowly, slowly he went in. Those were our only two points of contact – that hot, engorged knob ploughing its slow furrow into me and those maddeningly skilled teeth, working their wizardry on my true Mark of Submission. Oh, what need has he of the Six when he has found this One!

May 13th.
Who can tell the ways of the human mind? Nero's great fear in being so lenient with Bulbull, whom he merely dismissed from his service, has been totally overturned. He is, instead, a wise and powerful

leader, even more greatly to be feared than before! And what train of logic can lead to that?

Well, all the world knows that a eunuch cannot possibly have an erection or enjoy a woman; the entire harem 'business,' if one can call it that, is founded on the certainty. Therefore the woman who can induce such a condition in a man like Bulbull, and then take her pleasure from it, is surely supernatural. It follows that Bulbull is no more to blame for what happened than if I had turned him into a frog or a flying steed or something more usual and easy in that line. And what a wise man Nero Bey is in seeing at once where the true mischief lay!

What a powerful man, too. For did he not take me, this most dangerous of witches, and thrash me into subjection to his will – all heedless of the terrible magic I might have worked upon him? Did he not put Six *Thousand* Marks of Submission upon me? And do I not now meekly follow him into the Room of Joys each night and there lie with him in absolutely passive surrender to his lust? Aha! Truly he is not a man to cross, this Nero Bey. Next time he demands some favour, it would be only prudent to grant it.

This much truth there is in the common gossip: It is now me and me alone who is nightly chosen to lead that slim, vibrant black body into the Room of Joys. The others look on in envy, the two little monkeys with their all-seeing ears, Sulayah, with her wan face, Ouné, growing ever more desperate for the feel of her lord inside her again – and now Rosa, too, who is restored to favour in the general mood of amnesty.

But I feel no guilt as yet. I think of all those nights when I was the one who stood out there, longing for what I now receive in such abundance; and I think it will do their ultimate happiness no harm to face postponement for a season.

'You see?' Nero murmurs in my ear. 'Are we not of an older and wiser civilization? It is the woman's part to resist, to be shy, to submit in silence, to be passive, to receive her lord into her and accept whatever he offers her. And it is the man's role to ease aside the veils of her natural modesty – not with force but with the subtle kindness of desire – to hunt for her delights within her. Can you find such joys alone as you find with me?'

'No,' I whisper, and it is true.

'You see? It is I who find it there and make of it a gift for you. Have I not discovered delights even you did not suspect were there?'

He touches that spot, high on my backbone, and I shiver. 'Yes.'

'There you are. Now lie perfectly still and let us see what more treasures of bliss lie locked away in this sweet flesh of yours.'

Almost at once he finds a subtle blend of rhythms that is absolutely mine – quite different from the one he found for Rosa. We are lying on our side and he is into me from behind. He does not need to touch that spot on my back, nor my nipples nor my *bouton d'amour,* nor any of those electric parts of me. He just clasps my hips to stop each of his hard, hard thrusts from pushing me away. And because there is no other contact between us, all my energy, all my desires, are now focussed into that spellbound flesh, cradled between his hands. I feel the wicked curve of his long *poignard* as he enters and withdraws. I feel each fold and rille of my civet as she parts to accept him, rushes back to caress his retreat. And at last I am overwhelmed with that ancient pleasure.

But now I can hardly call it coming, for it does not pour over me in waves; it does not start here and ripple its thrills through me, petering out there; it

142

does not grip me with a force that shatters my breath and heartbeat. It is like nothing I have ever known before. I remember it as a kind of transformation of everything inside me, a bodily move – *all* of my body – into another land. I was suddenly made of a different kind of flesh, finer, lighter, with blood that sparkled like champagne. Time either stopped, or became infinite, or ceased to have meaning at all.

What when I 'came back to earth'? That is oddest of all. The experience has wrought a permanent change within me. I now live in total submission to Nero Bey; I cannot deny that. And yet, in some curious way, I feel more free than at any previous time in my life. Free not just of my past obsessions and prejudices but even of Nero himself. Am I the slave of my mind or is my mind the slave of me and all I experience? Those questions have as much meaning as: Am I the slave of Nero Bey or is he the slave of me?

For it would not be difficult to show that he *is* my slave, indeed. When I stood outside the Room of Joys and watched him with Ouné, I saw her passivity become, as I thought, a bottomless well that drew him in and made him evermore desperate to fill it. The more delight she discovered in that smiling submission of hers, the more violently he found himself working to increase it. All I saw then was that he was the slave and she the queen.

But now that I have learned to live in that same world, now that I see it from the inside, I realize what a shallow view that was. When the man and the woman accept their roles in this drama – *both* with absolute submission – then *both* are liberated to a precisely equal degree.

I suppose there will be no way of explaining this to people back in Paris next year!

Monday, June 24th, 1851.

It has taken us half a year but we seem to have

achieved it at last – the perfect balance in our little harem. We have no new eunuch yet – and no need of one either. Now that the factory is starting to fill with workers and clacking looms, Nero is hardly ever away. Nightly he wanders naked among us, picking his pleasure-companions for the night. Almost always the two little monkeys have their half-hour with him, passing from submission to frenzy to exhaustion. Then it is either Sulayah and Rosa or Ouné and me. I cannot say who is chosen more frequently nor who gets the lion's share of his loving. We no longer live in that book-keeping sort of world. All I can say is that six less nervous, frustrated, unfulfilled females never lived beneath one roof.

Nero has a masterly way of pleasuring two women at once so that neither feels the other is getting the best of it. The very sight of that beautiful curved *charrue* glistening with the juices from the other woman's *caverne,* is in itself a powerful thrill – because the onlooker knows it will soon be hers, too. When I lie on one part of the Venus Couch, watching him enter Ouné and withdraw, enter and withdraw – almost always full in and full out – I feel myself melting with a fever of anticipation; so that when he transfers to me I am ready to burst for him. And I glance across at her and see her lying there exactly as he left her, eyes lightly closed, and that enigmatic smile on her lips ... then I know she is in that other, timeless land to which he always returns. And then, though I can feel him entering me and withdrawing in that same way, I also feel, by some magical proxy, how the opened lips of *her* civet are already tingling for the renewed touch of him. Then I feel her joys added to my own. I cannot understand how Sulayah, for all those years, thought she and Nero were above such joy. She is in fact the one among us *least* able to submit and control her own feelings. I, who once almost cracked the Duke's plasterwork with my yells of delight (or so he grumbled), now burn with shame to hear how uninhibited she can be.

Wednesday, July 17th.
Poor Nero begins to flag. And who can wonder, the darling man. Keeping six such females happy, trained by him to expect the finest pleasuring in all the world, is impossible. If one of us is not soon got in child – or two or three of us – I fear for his health. It will not be me, of course, for I still take my Grandmother's precautions with that curious silver pego-cum-douche, which has so far saved me, as it did her for so many years, from that fate.

Also in two weeks' time Salome will be sixteen; her present is to be that marvellous black gristle – inside her at last! Poor Nero! Wonderful as it will be for all that training to bear fruit, he will now have yet another all-submissive, all-yielding, all-demanding dumb glutton for him to keep filled and happy.

But ... the choice was his, not ours.

Sunday, August 3rd, 1851.

The greatest day in little Salome's life! How she
hadn't died in sheer delirium before it even began,
I'll never know. On the eve of the sabbath, last
Friday, Nero withdrew from the harem to keep
himself in continence. For those two days we poor,
neglected women have been able to talk of little else
but Salome's surrender of her virginity – and even
had we wished to change the topic, she would not
have let us. She asked each of us to describe our own
deflowering. The answers surprised me. What they
tell us about 'love' in this continent, is less clear.

Rosa had lost her maidenhead to another woman in
the slave quarters at the age of twelve. Because of
the difficulty of getting men down there, a lot of that
sort of thing goes on among them.

Ouné, who had been intended for a brothel in Sidi-
el-Barrès before Nero discovered her, had hers broken deliberately and carefully by her future brothel
owner, using a lubricated ivory dildo. It had then
been stitched together again, because the panders
could more easily control the sale of them in that
way; with luck and careful management, a virgin's
'first time' could be sold to half a dozen deliriously
happy French officers during her first week in a truly
businesslike house.

They thought the way I had lost mine most bizarre
– but, knowing me, quite credible.

And Sulayah had lost hers to Nero Bey on the third
night of their week-long wedding feast. She remembers little of it, being so drugged with hashish by
then; her only clear memory was of her relatives
grabbing the bloodstained sheets from beneath her
and parading them in glory through the town.

As poor little Salome listened to our tales her face
grew longer and longer. But I soon cheered her up. I

said, 'You see in what miserable ways we all began!' (I did not consider my own way miserable but for her sake I pretended.) 'And yet we have all come to know such joys! How fortunate are you, then, Little Vixen, to be deflowered by the man you love most in all the world – and a man who is without doubt the finest lover of women that any of us knows!'

I do not think she slept at all last night. We spent the entire afternoon bathing her, dressing her hair, and rubbing oil and perfume into her skin. Five different perfumes she had – on her neck, in her hair, under her arms, on her breasts, and between her thighs. Sulayah spent much of that time painting her feet and lower legs with henna, making elaborate designs on her skin; then the same on her forearms, from her wrists to her elbows. The effect, I have to admit, was powerfully erotic – something of which we had to keep reassuring the young bride, who could feel it but not see it, of course.

Tonight there was no division of Nero's time among us into 'social' and 'sexual' – it was straight into the Room of Joys for the happy pair as soon as he came up. We all gathered at the wall to watch and admire – and envy. Nero was naked as usual. Salome was dressed in a deep blue silken tunic and pants, this time with no opening between her thighs. The first thing he had to do was calm her down; she was in such a state of anticipation by then that we all feared an outburst of hysterics.

He laid her gently on her back and caressed her lips with grapes – except that sometimes it was not grapes but his own lips and tongue. And all the while he stroked her hair and cuddled her neck with the backs of his fingers. When she seemed quite calm again, he began to unbutton her tunic and reach those feather-light fingers inside to play with her breasts. He opened her tunic and spread it wide, leaning over her to kiss her breasts and tease them with his tongue. Then he straddled her and, taking her little nipples between thumb and forefinger, squeezed them gently, in about the rhythm of a normal heartbeat.

She grew excited again, of course, but not in that dangerous, uncontrolled way. Instead it was that deep, interior excitement that we women knew so well but which we had never before seen in either of the little monkeys. Ah me – I cannot call her 'little monkey' any longer now!

When he saw her afloat on that deep lake of contentment, Nero moved to her side and turned her over, taking her tunic right off as she turned. He eased down those little trousers until they were about her hips. The pillow on which her lower half lay was large and white. I had never seen it before but, remembering Sulayah's tale, I had no difficulty in guessing its purpose. Salome crossed her arms under a smaller pillow of brown velvet, on which she laid her head. Then he moved one hand in under her little breasts again while he placed the other flat on the small of her back. And with each of those marvellous hands moving in different, subtle ways, he began a long, gentle massage – not caressing her hips and little *derrière* but simply moving the skin in the small of her back gently over the bone beneath.

This morning she told me that the sensation which flowed out from both those magic hands was like 'flames of ice, tingling all through me.'

Slowly he eased the pants down, caressing her in ever widening circles and lines and diagonals ... no two circuits of that sweetly tormented young flesh were the same. When all her bottom was bare, and we could just see the back ends of her engorged

148

labia, I suddenly realized how womanly her proportions had become in just these past few weeks.

Down went those magic fingers, into the perfumed cleft between her shivering thighs. When he brought it out it gleamed with her juice. There was now no point in delaying any longer.

He removed her trousers right down over her ankles and, placing one of his knees between hers, eased them apart. She did nothing until he led her into it. His other knee followed, making her spread herself wider yet. We could see both her labia, hot and scarlet with their hunger for the touch of him, which was now so close.

That awesomely curved organ of his, burnished black and gleaming with his own excited secretions, was so stiff I thought he would have to lift her upright, almost standing her up, to get it in. But he grasped her hips between those great, gentle hands and lifted her *derrière* to him. I wanted to cry out, 'No! Let her watch it go in!' Then I remembered!

He leaned forward over her, pushing his ebon rod down between her parted thighs. She was so small compared to him that, although they were now both in the same, almost triangular shape, her curves fitted snugly inside his; and their touch was gentle from their knees to their heads. The upper side of his *couteau* made a long, sliding caress of her rosebud; at once she whimpered with happiness. After a few more slow strokes in that fashion, I could see the sweat break out on her back and there were blushes all over her skin.

He took her hand and guided it up between her thighs. She understood at once that she was to play with his *joujou* – the sensitive underside of his knob – as she wished, and then help guide him into her. I think I never saw anything more delicately done. She caressed and tickled him until he made urgent, warning noises in his throat, and then, thrusting her *derrière* up against him as hard as she possibly could, she got his knob against the lips of her wide-open fig. And there, guiding him imperceptibly by little moans and catches of her breath, and wriggling her hips in a slow sort of spasm, she allowed him into her at last. Any sigh she might have made was drowned for us by a great, collective sigh of our own. It was done at last; the girl had become a woman.

Then he went into her all the way – not the full length of his weapon but to the very root of her *canal d'amour;* even so, I was astonished at the length she was able to accept. In two or three years time she will be the only wife he has who can take all of him in without discomfort. He stayed there for a time without moving, while she hollowed her back and tried to bend her *canal* to the curve of him.

The movement gave her one mighty climax that took her utterly by surprise. It must have rushed up inside her from nowhere, overwhelming all her defences, all her training. She gave out cry after cry of joy.

Little Sherry slipped her hand into mine and squeezed. I looked at her and saw the tears running down her face. Poor little mite! So ready for the pleasures of Venus in her mind, so prepared in her body – and so many long months to wait until her body may taste those exquisite joys!

Nero asked Salome if she wished to stop and rest awhile but she said no, she wanted him to go on to his own climax; she wanted to feel him spending into her at long, long last.

He spun it out for her as long as he could; every move he made seemed to bring her back to that plateau where each thrust was a new rapture, each retreat a fresh bliss. At last, when she was bathed in sweat and fighting for her breath, he made three quick thrusts and gave out a great roar of joy. Even we could see it. The inch or two of *cervelas* that was still outside her body throbbed and pulsed like a mad firehose under the enormous pressure of his ejaculations. I think she was actually knocked unconscious with the ecstasy of it and if she had not been impaled upon the mighty spar of his flesh, she would have keeled over, I'm sure.

For any other young girl just turned sixteen, that would have been more than enough. But Salome was by now such a veteran of joys with him that for her, their night of bliss had just begun. More grapes, a little sherbet, and they were entwined in their pleasuring again – and then again – and then again.

One by one we watchers outside slunk to our beds to curse the ill fate that had lost us our maidenheads in such inept or casual ways – even Sulayah, I think, for Nero was not then the lover we and others have made him since.

The following morning the telltale pillow was carried through the palace like the spoils of war, and everyone who saw it cheered to the echo. And what a different Salome we saw! Those dry-as-dust clerics who preach celibacy and chastity for those unfortunate women who must live without men should be forced to see her now – and then try to explain that new lustre to her skin, the new delicacy and grace of her movements, her growing awareness of and pleasure in the power of her charms, and the deep pool of understanding that now seems to lie behind those sightless eyes. Could any better proof be desired that we are created by a truly loving God to give and take carnal pleasure with our bodies; all else is a mere filling-out of time.

[*FR: From here on, the remaining diary entries are scant. Fanny, who could so vividly record all the changes in her sexual odyssey, obviously found it impossible to record a state of perfect bliss that just goes on and on in ... well, a state of perfect bliss. She tries to compensate for it by describing her work in the new carpet factory, where she set up an entire photographic department and trained several of Nero Bey's slaves in the techniques it offered. There are also fascinating travelogue-like descriptions of her expeditions into the town and the semi-desert all around. The story of her sexual development does not pick up again until the eve of her departure, on her return to Paris. It was delayed at her own pleading, until almost the end of March 1852 – a three-month freebie for Nero Bey! He seems to have borne it well. Her actual departure was dry-eyed, for they both knew that any time he was in Paris, he'd once again rule her with his rod of ebony, all night long.*

Fanny took Ouné with her. The ease with which Nero agreed to the arrangement reveals, perhaps, that a female who demands her pleasures on such a scale and so frequently is not the stuff of Everyman's dreams, after all. Alas, the pages that describe their return to Paris have been ripped from the only edition I have; even more maddeningly, they have been only three-quarters ripped, so that one can still make out something of what they contained. First came an argument with the Duke, who, notwithstanding his earlier protestations of undying love for Fanny, flatly refused to take her back.

I suspect he had been got at by the Countess, who wanted her now-experienced granddaughter to join in the management of the de C. sex-empire. The torn stubs of the pages hint at arguments on that score, too. The Countess wished Fanny to spend a season as une grande horizontale, *one of Vallodon's fillies, in fact – even though it would put her in the strange position of*

working for herself. But Fanny – and Ouné – were
determined to try the Game at a much humbler level.
And, as you are about to learn, they prevailed. A grande
horizontale, like any high-class call girl, was expected to
limit her clientèle to one gentleman a day, and to give
him her all. One suspects that was not nearly exciting
enough for our two young nymphs – not that Fanny
would have put it so bluntly to her grandmother. A
surviving snippet in the mutilated pages gives a clue to
her argument with the old dame; it was couched in the
dramatic form Fanny always used for those particular
conversations:

ME: I know I shall hate it, but ...

That's all – but enough, surely? From it, and some of
her later, surviving, comments, we may surmise that,
being a thoroughgoing Victorian miss, Fanny concealed
her pleasure beneath a mask of stern duty. How sincere
she was the reader may judge from her concluding
remarks in this little memoir – which may also explain
why she felt obliged to rip out those pages where her
hypocrisy was only too apparent.

Her narrative resumes as the two girls begin their new
trade at one of the de C. houses for young girls, called
the Maison d'Or.]

Tuesday, May 4th.
I had not realized how important one's own name
and history can be. When I shed mine this morning
and became Jenny Diver, a little ruin'd maid sacked
from a hotel, I felt an awful drabness enter my soul.
Ouné says my whole body changed – and it wasn't
just the ill-fitting clothes I bought off a rather startled
room maid at our hotel. My shoulders drooped, my
head hung forward. I looked as if I had not slept –

well, that, at least, was true! Anyway, it certainly was not the Hon. Fanny Duplessis who knocked so hesitantly at the door of the Maison d'Or at two o'clock this afternoon. Ouné, of course, was almost wetting herself with excitement by then.

Mme Dutourd also has two faces – one is of great charm, which she turns toward her customers; the other is one of stern mistrust. It was an even grimmer version of this second face that greeted Ouné and me inside her private parlour.

'Very well,' she snapped, only waiting to take in half our mumbled story – which, naturally, she must have heard a thousand times before. 'Go in there and take off your clothes – all of them.'

We shivered in an opulently furnished yet somehow cheerless bedroom for about five minutes before a dishevelled old man came in, nodded cheerily to us, and said, 'On the bed, little darlings – flat on your backs, if you please.' I thought this might be some milder form of Vallodon's test and smiled at him encouragingly. He laughed. 'You can save that, my pet. This is just your medical examination. I am your doctor while you're here. We'll meet in these amiable circumstances every Tuesday morning.'

We had to lie on the bed and hug our knees to our bosoms while he poked around down there with speculums and things. Then we stood up and showed him our tongues and said 'Ah!' and he seemed quite satisfied. Mme Dutourd came in as he was packing up. 'Well?' she asked.

'Fresh and clean. Two healthy young wenches who have been enjoying a good bit of traffic, I'd say, but not in trade. No sign of it in their anuses, at least.'

Mme Dutourd nodded grimly. 'There's none of that here, anyway. No hair, I see.'

'Plucked,' he told her.

Her smile said she'd managed to work that out for herself. 'Good,' she said approvingly to us. 'Most of our *poulettes* are plucked here. The men prefer it. We have a couple with a bit of a frizz, just for the variety.'

She ignored his departure and turned to inspect us minutely. I felt like some poor beast in a market, which I suppose I now was. Her scrutiny softened her mood a little. I could see we represented something of a catch for her modest establishment – though she was determined not to show it. Anyway, the upshot was that we were taken on for a week's trial. Normally that would mean kicking out two girls, but the warm spring weather was driving the men of Paris wild and the Maison d'Or could actually do with a couple more yet; so, until she got them, we'd be 'doing' ten to fifteen customers a day and two dozen on Saturdays and Sundays. We'd work straight on through our monthlies; she'd show us how when the time came.

Since the Countess had led me to expect I'd be 'doing' two dozen every day, this was something of a relief. Did the old girl know it, the clever thing?

Mme Dutourd told us we needn't work this afternoon. We could settle into our rooms – which would be our working rooms as well – and talk to the other young *poulettes*. 'They'll tell you all the rules and how to comport yourselves with our customers,' she said. 'And they'll also tell you I expect unquestioning obedience. So away you go – and make sure you're in the salon at six sharp – bathed, perfumed, and undressed ready for service.'

Our rooms are almost identical; Ouné's and mine have a connecting door, which is nice. The entire house is pervaded by the smells of stale cigar smoke, cheap perfume, and the bodies of young girls. To our customers, I suppose, it must be very stimulating. The furnishings are cheap  and showy. We each have a huge bed of gilded plaster with a deep feather mattress and umpteen pillows and cushions. The other standard furnishings and contents are: a long mirror with a slight tint of rose in the glass; a smaller oval mirror facing it; a washstand and chamberpot and douche (but I shall use my own, from my grandmother); a cupboard full of bed-linen, which the maids change after every two customers (my heart sank when I counted enough for fifteen changes); a velvet-upholstered *chaise-longue*; a padded chair without arms; and a curiously hump-backed little padded stool with two-inch legs, rising to about six inches high.

Yvette, one of the other girls, came to welcome us during our unpacking – which was scant, of course. She is eighteen, of average height with frizzy blonde hair. She was almost naked, about to step into her bath, I supposed, and I could see through the loose

folds of her gown that she was very slender, with small, pointed breasts – almost perfect cones, in fact. 'Welcome to Paradise,' she said sarcastically.

'What's it really like?' I inquired.

'Where have you worked before?'

'Nowhere.'

'Oh.' Her face fell.

'Is it rough?' I asked.

'Are you virgins?'

We grinned sheepishly.

'Well, at least *that* bit's over!' Yvette smiled. 'I must go.'

'Yes, we mustn't keep you from your bath.'

She looked down at her gown and laughed. 'Bath! No, darling, I'm *jour* this afternoon. These are our glad rags. The gentlemen all like to have a good grope before they buy. See you this evening. When you've unpacked, pop down to our boudoir and have a chat with Geraldine. She's the best one to put you straight – if that's quite the word for it!'

Ouné's eyes followed her out enviously. I sat on that vast, seductively soft bed and wondered what awful encounters I was going to have to endure there before my month in this house was over.

Half an hour later we drifted into the 'boudoir,' a room of faded elegance overlooking the narrow back yard. The windows are tall and frosted – no free glimpses of Paradise at the Maison d'Or. The smell of powder, perfume, and females was almost over-powering. Two maids, stolid women in their thirties, were sitting there playing a simple card game. The only *poulettes de joie* present were called Franchine and Blanche. They, too, were dressed for the salon. We introduced ourselves. Blanche, who was nineteen, was filing her nails. She said, 'Thank God for some relief. My hole was starting to wear away.'

The two maids laughed. She said it was all very well for them, they hadn't been doing two dozen filthy cocks a day for the past five thousand years.

I said Yvette had advised us to have a talk with Geraldine. Blanche asked what the hell we imagined that one could tell us that our own worst forebodings couldn't? But Franchine, a buxom, pneumatic girl of sixteen, with short, dark hair, gave us a reassuring nod and slipped out of the room.

Blanche is tall and slim with curly, chestnut-brown hair. She has large, soft breasts, a slender waist, and very wide hips considering her general proportions. But something about her made me uneasy. She asked where we'd worked before. We told her nowhere. She looked at the ceiling and whistled; but then she cast a decidedly predatory eye over Ouné.

Franchine returned with Geraldine, who looked to me about eighteen. She was dressed for the street, as were we. She is a lovely looking redhead with a freckled face and the friendliest of smiles. Her thin, sensitive lips and gentle eyes inspired complete trust. 'I was just going out shopping,' she said. 'Would you care to join me? We can go to the Palais Royal and take coffee and talk to our heart's content.'

'Without every word going straight back to madame,' Blanche said. 'I know.'

When we were outdoors Geraldine confessed that her shopping trip was a ruse to get away from the place. I asked if it was so odious. She said not at all but she didn't care too much for some of the people. Blanche especially. She was the 'house spy' and carried every bit of gossip to madame. Arlette, whom we had not yet met, was madame's other favourite – be careful with her, too. However, she added that though madame was stricter than any sergeant-major, she was also very fair and just.

We told her our (invented) stories on the way.

'Well,' she said when we were sipping our coffees, 'I suppose the best thing to begin with is to tell you our usual routine. First you should know that the Maison d'Or is a very bourgeois house. You know that the houses of the Comte de C. are of three main kinds – for the workers, for the *bourgeoisie,* and some very special ones for the *haute monde?'*

'We know nothing of these matters,' I replied.

'In the workers' houses the girls are not at all appetizing. They sit in numbered rooms, very simply furnished. The customers pay two francs at the door and get given a threadbare towel and the number of a room — no choice. The time allowed is about ten minutes. The girl gets one franc. In all the C. houses the division is half-and-half. On a really busy night a girl there can do fifty customers, so her pay could almost equal ours for a moderately hard night, when we might do fifteen. We earn three francs fifty per client, plus tips — and a generous or well-satisfied customer can easily give five francs by way of a tip, so the money is good.' She smiled at us both. 'Keep telling yourselves that tonight: The money is good and the Comte de C. is a very fair employer.'

'Is it really so awful otherwise?' I asked.

She patted my hand. 'It's worse than you may hope but it's better than you feared. It depends so much on your attitude. Blanche and Arlette hate men; they  are quite indifferent to the work and it has no effect on their spirit. I love men. I adore them in all their vanity, all their pomposity, all their uncertainty. If I get a run of nice ones, I feel it's the most marvellous work in all the world. If I get a run of the crude, the careless, the vulgar, the indifferent, then I'm Madame Misery herself. All in all, though, I'm happy enough. I'm not like poor Jacqui, who's only just sixteen and has never yet responded to a man and really, I think, has no idea what she's doing here. It's only that she's so beautiful that she gets away with it.

Men look at a beautiful woman lying naked on the bed and they fill to bursting with their own lust. They can never believe it's only *their* lust. Because that woman inspired it, they think she must feel it, too. That's young Jacqui's secret.' She smiled at Ouné. 'You'll be the same. You could actually sleep through half your encounters and they'll swear you almost died of your desire for them!'

'I won't sleep!' Ouné assured her.

'What about the aristocratic houses?' I asked.

'Ah! Now in those places the girls really earn their ... well, it begins at twenty francs and goes up as high as you like. In those houses anything goes. His lordship wishes to enter by the back passage? She squeals with delight as he prods away. He wants to whip her senseless? She cannot wait for him to tear the clothes off her back.

A little preliminary love affair with her mouth is a standard offering there. And there are things even more bizarre. In fact, nothing is forbidden as long as it is handsomely paid for. I could never work in one of those places!'

My spirit rose at this news. 'Then certain things *are* forbidden at the Maison d'Or?'

'Oh yes, quite a lot. We're not just a *bourgeois* house, we are *une maison de poulettes* – every girl aged between sixteen and twenty.' She winked at us. 'Though, between ourselves, you understand, some of us are only here because we pass for that age still. Anyway, gentlemen come to the Maison d'Or for a fresh, clean, near-innocent young *poulette* – which is what we magically become when we enter the salon. If they ask us to suck them off or give a bit of brown, we must act horrified at the very thought. If they want that, they must go to the aristocratic houses – although they can get *soixante-neuf* in the other bourgeois houses, where the women are over twenty, the *maisons de poules.*'

'Who lays down such rules?' I asked, having a very good idea of the answer.

'I believe it was the Countess herself. Years ago there was a lot of trouble in the *maisons de poulettes,* and she made these laws. Only nice clean fun for us!'

'Why that mocking tone, Geraldine?' I asked.

'I think it's a clever way of breaking us slowly to the trade. Our useful life in the C. houses is extended by it. When we are twenty, we're fully broken and ready for anything. No hysterics.' She grinned. 'Anyway – the rules are: no anal traffic. No *soixante-neuf* ... you do know what that is, *hein?*'

We nodded.

Her eyebrows arched up. 'Oh, do you? What's going on in the hotels of Paris these days, I wonder? Soon the men won't bother coming to us at all! What else is not allowed? No whipping, of course. Mind you, if they want to give you a bit of boisterous spanking, and you can get a lot more money out of them for it – well, nobody minds that. I'm quite fond of a bit of spanking myself, with the right sort of fellow. But there's no shitting or pissing on them or letting them chew your stockings and knickers. If you offer any of these forbidden services, you lose all that week's earnings and you're out on your *con*. That's a very strict rule of the Count's. If anyone asks for such things, refer him politely to Mme Dutourd, who has a complete list of the aristocratic houses and knows how to send him on his way with his tail up.'

'Who are these men?' I asked. 'I mean what sort of *normal* men frequent us?'

She shrugged. 'The *bourgeoisie*, of course. Doctors, lawyers, people in trade ... professional people. A lot of clerics – they come in disguise but you get to know after a while. The rest are all married, ninety-five out of a hundred, I'd say. It's enough to put you off marriage, don't you think?'

'Students?' Ouné asked hopefully. 'Officers?'

'A few students. Lots of officers. They can be fun, the younger ones. Students can get a bit soulful. They want you to *love* them, too. And they've no money.'

She smiled. We must have looked a little woebegone for she said, 'Cheer up, all you *really* have to do is make each customer feel you only started in the trade yesterday and he's the best lover you've had since then. Fake a climax when you feel him beginning to rise to his. If you can squeeze your *vagin* while he's spending, that'll send him away happy.'

'And do you always *fake* a climax?' Ouné asked.

Geraldine laughed. 'I can't set too many hopes flying in that direction, my dear. And never talk about coming with customers when the other girls are around. They think it's disgusting. Or at least, they pretend to. It's a sort of bravado among us – only

163

men are weak in that way – we're above it. Actually, I think most of them are like me.'

'And you do ... I mean you don't always fake them?' I asked.

She shook her head. 'But it's not the way you may think. The most gorgeous young officer can leave you absolutely cold, whereas a fif-ty-year-old fatty with a prick like a small pencil can occasionally light a fire inside you.  Don't ask me the whys and wherefores. It just happens. It's a little bit extra. Very nice. But don't expect it to happen often. And above all, never let a customer leave you thinking he *didn't* light a genuine fire inside you. I think it's sweet of men to care about our feelings so much. I'm sure if I was a man, paying for *une fille de joie,* I wouldn't care two hoots for her pleasure as long as she did everything to increase mine. But men are like that – sweet, deluded, sentimental, warm-hearted darlings!' She looked at a clock hanging over the café door. 'We should be thinking of getting back. We get a light meal now, then ... bath ... perfume and powder ... and working dress. What have you got? Never mind, I can lend you something. Remember – just ... generally keep smiling and look voluptuous and – oh, neither of you is going to have any trouble. I can see that already. Unless ...' She hesitated and looked at me.

'What?' I asked.

'D'you *like* men, Jenny?' she asked me suddenly.

My unfamiliar name caught me off guard. I'm sure she knows it's false now.

'I don't mean sex,' she added. 'Not lying in bed, coupled together. But *men*. D'you like them?'

I stared at her in amazement. 'D'you know,' I said. 'I honestly have no idea!'

She laughed. 'Good for you! Well, you've come to the best place in the world to find out.'

I bathed and powdered myself as in a dream. All I could think of was that very soon now, some unknown and probably unlovely man was going to walk into this house and buy the right to pull me upstairs, take off my clothes and thrust himself into me, and I'd have to pretend to be thrilled by it all, no matter how dreadful he was. I remembered boasting to the Duke about the feelings that would delight me if I ever had to take up this trade – the power to draw completely unknown men to my room ... and all that. I tried to feel even one shred of that excitement now, but it was all gone. That was fantasy. Here I was up to the neck in fact.

My working attire, partly lent by Geraldine, consists of: pale pink slippers with my toes peeping out; ribbed white silk stockings held just above the knee by peach-coloured garters of satin; a loosely tied bust bodice with lace that just shields my nipples, preserving a coy sort of indecent decency; and a loose, flowing chemise with lace flounces around the hem which just reach my knees. The whole effect is one of available innocence, which is what the *maisons de poulettes* are selling.

As she helped me arrange these garments, Geraldine said, 'Remember, never adopt a pose that is openly lascivious when you're in the salon. Firstly, it is against the policy of the house. Secondly, such poses are a great strain and if you force the other girls to compete with you, we all get very tired. Thirdly, and most important of all, some customers are regulars for one girl and if she's working when they call, they wait until she becomes available. If they were seduced by you in some voluptuous pose, that would create bad blood. Just sit looking demure and slightly ... I don't know ... fluttery. You'll see.'

Our fingernails, teeth, and breath passed Mme Dutourd's muster and we crowded forward into the salon. 'I'll pick you a nice one to start on,' the old dragon promised me kindly as I passed her.

There were four or five gentlemen already waiting – regulars, Geraldine murmured to me. This moment, when half a dozen freshly bathed young *poulettes* came nervously in was especially exciting to them. I know the one I would have picked: a young officer with a monocle (and a twinkle) in his eye – which was already looking me up and down delightedly. I touched madame's arm to whisper my choice to her but, to my dismay, she took me directly to a short, fat man of at least fifty, with pince-nez, a huge, untidy beard, and no hair.

'Monsieur d'Alembert,' she cooed, 'see what I have for you tonight – the most beauteous English rose, quite new to the game. Will you be kind and gentle with her, eh? I know you will, my dear old friend.'

His eyes were popping out of his head at his luck. 'Come, leetle flower,' he said in English. 'We seet a beet first, hein?'

He led me to one of the sofas. Ouné passed me, hauling my young officer toward the door; they were almost tripping over each other in their eagerness to be alone. I smiled my warmest smile at M d'Alembert and told him my name was Jenny and I could, in fact, speak perfect French. The news appeared to delight him still further.

'And is this truly your first time?' he asked, slipping a hand into my chemise and feeling my breasts.

'Well ... you understand, M'sieu, I'm no virgin.'

He laughed. 'No! I think madame would have made more fuss if it had been that!' His hand was pulling at the strings of my bust bodice, which were but loosely tied.

I put an arm about him and stroked his head. 'I'm glad she picked out you,' I assured him, hoping I sounded sincere. 'Mature men are so ...'

He grinned and pulled his hand out a moment to waggle a finger at me. 'I think the young officer would have pleased you more. But' – he winked and tapped the side of his nose – 'just compare notes with your pretty young friend after!' His hand burrowed inside my chemise again and began doing quite expert things with my breasts. Actually, now that I came to look at him closely, I could see he must have been quite a handsome man in his day. I stretched and threw out my chest, inviting more, giving a deep sigh of contentment.

He was watching me closely and I knew he was trying to see how genuine my responses were; the trouble was, even I could not have told him. They were not entirely genuine, of course; but nor were they entirely fake. I saw that if a girl cared to work at it, she might derive much pleasure in this trade

His hand went down to my hairless crevice and proved equally at home there with a girl's springs of joy. My heart raced. 'What do you do, M d'Alembert?' I asked unsteadily

'I supply wine to your country, my dear. The best.'

'I think you are a man who is used to only the best,' I murmured, kissing him warmly.

'I think you supply it, too,' he replied gently.

'But you'd better be quick,' I went on, 'or it's all going to happen down here.'

Incredibly – it must have been the fever of my nerves, the agony of our preparations, and my relief at finding him a far nicer man than had at first appeared possible – incredibly I was almost coming down there in the salon, within a few minutes of meeting my first customer!

While he gave Mme Dutourd his seven francs (they can pay either her or us), Geraldine murmured to me, 'You'll like him. And remember – there are twenty-thousand other women doing exactly this in Paris tonight, probably a thousand of them at exactly this moment.'

We seemed to float upstairs, me ahead of him and making my hips sway as Geraldine had advised: 'You can get him half-way there before he's even reached the landing!'

When we were in my room he straight away took out his pego and held it expectantly toward me in one hand – like some sort of gift. The trouble with Geraldine's attempt to comfort me is that when the door shuts behind you, it doesn't matter how many or how few sisters you have out there, lying on their backs, there's only one Polyphemus looking at you with its ravenous red eye; and there's only one soft, warm, juicy little *dévorant* can gratify its appetite.

I frowned in bewilderment; I had forgotten I was supposed to look at it for chancre and things. He reminded me and then laughed. 'You're safe enough,' he assured me, starting to undress himself in earnest. 'I never go anywhere but here. And always on a Tuesday, straight after the medical. You're supposed to be undressing me, by the way – folding my clothes, and so on.' He sat on the bed and waited.

As I finished undressing him he told me of his reactions. 'The sight of a very pretty, very young girl like you, my dear, folding my clothes and smoothing them with your pale, slim fingers is highly voluptuous. Now I hope you will make all your movements lascivious and slow ...'

I pulled off his long underpants to reveal his pego again, quite a respectable thing, half hidden beneath his great paunch. I stared at it, longingly, I hope.

He got me to put a great pile of pillows at the edge of the bed. Then he bent me gently forward over them. He had arranged them in such a way that my breasts hung into a space among them. Then he adjusted both the mirrors and, without further ceremony or talk, pushed his gristle deep into my cleft. As I said, it was of a respectable size, so he could make it take quite a while going in and out. He watched it all in the mirror. As he was nowhere near coming, I made only the slightest little moans of happiness – just one or two drawn-out sighs of 'Oooooh!'. Whether he was truly deceived or not, it seemed to give him great pleasure.

He changed his rhythm slightly and began to caress my breasts, pinching the nipples gently in time with his rodding. My sighs became a little more genuine.

'Good!' He withdrew, leapt over the pillows with astonishing agility, and lay flat on his back with his big wet tool throbbing in the air. He put down a hand to hold it still. 'You go on top now,' he said.

I quite liked that, too – being able to control the pace and depth of each stroke. In any other circumstances, I'd have had a couple of climaxes by now, but, although I seemed always to be hovering close to one, it just wouldn't come.

Soon after that he lay me on my back, across the edge of the bed and with my feet on the floor. He stood up, pushed my thighs wide apart, and rammed himself sharply inside me, to the very butt of him; luckily I was just long enough to take it but I gave a gasp and used that to start faking my climax. The trouble was, I was so close to a real one, the tension was becoming unbearable. Something was holding him back, too. I took a chance and pulled myself away from him. 'Here!' he cried, not at all pleased.

I crawled up the bed like an upside down crab and lay in the traditional position, on my back, thighs well parted. 'Come on,' I said eagerly. 'I'm so close to coming it's driving me wild. I want to feel the weight of you on me. Really hard.'

'I'll suffocate you,' he objected.

But I could not be stopped. 'No you won't, not if you're quick. It's what you want, too. I can feel it. Trust me, monsieur. Be hard and quick.'

I was right. With a cry of delight he lowered himself gently upon me and started poking away, full tilt.

He was right, too – he did very nearly suffocate me. But that soft, warm weight of him was exactly what I had needed and I spilled over in the most delicious confusion of juices and feelings that was very nearly as good as one of the dozens of preliminary *plaisirs* I used to have with Nero.

So it wasn't a bad start at all!

M d'Alembert let it soak a good long time – until I began to struggle for breath. Then he rolled to one side and lay on his back, gasping, 'Fantastic!'

I leaped on him and kissed his face all over and thanked him prettily for making my first time such a pleasure. He gave me five francs by way of a tip and said, 'You don't need any perfume, Mademoiselle Jenny, but buy some anyway and use it for me. I'll come sniffing around your lovely young body at the same time next week.'

Five minutes later, douched and repowdered, I was back in the salon ready to take on the whole *bourgeois* world.

If only they had all been like d'Alembert! I hardly arrived back in the salon before a tall, thin man grabbed me by the wrist and said, 'You'll do very nicely. Come on, I haven't much time.' He ran upstairs ahead of me, plonked seven francs on my dressing table, held out his horn, pulled it away before I'd had a proper chance to inspect it – all I saw was a medium-sized thing, rather bent and knobbly but otherwise clean and healthy-looking.

I started to undress him but he said, 'Don't fuss with all that, mam'selle. Just lie on the edge of the bed with your feet on the floor. No, no – leave all your clothes on. Quickly!'

He poked away in me for a couple of minutes, changing the pace every now and then and watching himself in the tall mirror. I started to sigh and moan. 'You can cut out all that,' he said. 'Just lie absolutely still and don't make a sound. Put your heels up on my shoulders now. Toes behind my head.'

He rodded me in that position, showing pleasure but no great excitement. At the end he got slower and slower and then finished in a tremendous burst of speed that took me by surprise. Then he withdrew and bowed – which tucked his limp gristle back inside his trousers for him – thanked me, and left.

It was nine minutes, salon-to-salon. Mme Dutourd frowned severely and came over to me. 'You didn't use any tricks to hurry him on?' she asked sharply.

I told her what had happened.

Her suspicions were not stilled, though. 'I won't stand for it again,' she snapped. 'We give all our customers a nice twenty minutes to half an hour.'

I almost burst into tears. What more did she want? Couldn't she understand what degradation and turmoil I was going through already, without feeling her eyes stabbing me in the back all the time?

'Well, miss,' she barked – the only ogress I know who can bark under her breath. 'Back to your duties, if you please! There's a customer over there with his eye on you – and if he leaves this house before the next half hour is out, you'll be docked ten francs. So pull yourself together.'

The fellow got his half-hour all right, to the minute. He was another silent man, a priest, I think, in his thirties. He simply wanted me to lie in position after position and act ecstatic all the time – sort of religious-ecstatic with my palms pressed together and my eyes on heaven. He nearly came in each position, stopping himself just in time (from his point of view). In the end, when I saw the hand on the clock tick past the magic moment, I milked him off with my *coquille* just when he wasn't expecting it – faking the most enormous climax for myself, and really not feeling a thing except relief at the spillage going on inside me. I glanced at Mme Dutourd the moment I returned to the salon – not challengingly I hope. I think I was allowed a millimetre of a smile for about one thousandth of a second. But fancy being docked ten francs – all my brilliant work so far this evening, all would have gone for nothing!

I don't remember the next two or three or four or however many it was. In fact, everything was a bit hazy from then on. I worked in the salon from 6pm to 3 in the morning; no one wanted an all-night with me, thank God. In that time I did fifteen customers. Now that I write the figure, I realize that until tonight, my body has played hostess to only nine men – and now in one night I have done nearly double that! Worse, I got so little pleasure by it. My last customer, at half past two, was the sweetest young student. If M. Vallodon had matched me with him, we should have had the greatest joy together – but by then I had nothing left to give. No, that is not true. All I had left to give was my finest acting skill; for him, I manufactured the most stupendous climax of the evening. And as it shivered and trembled all over the shell of me, I felt my inside all numb.

Twelve hours ago I could not have imagined a man inside me without stirring something – even disgust. But now ... all those men ... some with fine cocks and pleasing bodies ... nothing!

I see what Geraldine means about men. They are sweet, kind people, most of them. Of those fifteen, at least ten truly cared about my pleasure. 'What is your favourite position, mam'selle?' they asked, and 'Is there something *you* especially like doing?' And they work so hard at giving me thrills. They caress me in all the right places, they are gentle and loving ... and the most I feel is the glow of good companionship. That's it! The best they can truly hope to be for me is a good companion, letting me escape the worst of this vile business, giving me an easy time.

If that is sad, then how much sadder is the fact that I actually wish for nothing more. In the past, when I thought about this trade – while reading my grand-mother's letters, for instance – I'd say to myself, 'A dozen men in a night! You could try taking pleasure of them all, and even if you didn't succeed, you'd get near it with many, which is the next-best thing – and surely there'd be at least *one* who'd light a fire inside?' But it isn't like that, I find. Perhaps it will change as I grow more accustomed to it? At the moment, any hint of sexual thrill within me is an annoying intrusion. I want to learn to please these men, not to take accidental pleasure from them. Everything I do while they are poking me must be done because I decide to do it, not because some accidental jolt of electricity has stirred up my insides. When that happens, I lose some measure of my self-control ... I abandon my body to the old powers, the compulsive demands, of orgy and chaos.

Tomorrow, I shall go below with the right attitude. I shall become a professional.

I forgot to talk to Ouné about her experiences; and now she has an all-night customer.

I earned fr52.50 plus fr29 in tips. My five beautiful swans earned fr63 in that same time. The best of both worlds?

Wednesday, May 5th.
Ouné says the dashing young officer with the monocle had a long, thin ramrod, which he delighted in ramming against the top of her *canal* – not hard enough to hurt badly (he is too clever for that) but enough to cause great discomfort, which is his chief source of delight. He chooses to *enconner* that rapier of his with us *poulettes* because our *concons* are still small and he can hurt us more easily. Fortunately, madame says, there are not many with such warped minds – not among our regular custom, so we just have to grin and bear the odd one. She does not include herself, of course. Two girls here have *vagins* too long for him – Geraldine and, believe it or not, our youngest *poulette,* Jacqui! He never chooses them. Yvette told us some tricks to stop him – and any other men with long pricks – from pushing themselves all the way home inside us.

The rest of Ouné's customers were 'marvellous,' she says. She's in seventh heaven here, of course. Her

174

successive customers are actually one ideal Customer who can go on and on all night; and she just lies there with her eyes closed and that seraphic smile on her face, goading them to give her yet more thrills ... exactly the effect she had on Nero in the beginning.

Madame took us aside after breakfast – Ouné and me – to say, in a tone of gruff reluctance, that the opinion of the customers was that we'd been 'satisfactory' for beginners. 'But if they say any such nonsense to you,' she went on grimly, 'ignore it, don't let it turn your heads. It's all too easy to become slipshod in this work. Men are such deceivers, as we all know. What we don't realize is that they are their own worst victims.'

Our breakfast is at noon. I no longer notice the smell of female bodies. I love the other girls. We are all such jolly company when there are no men around. They were quite interested in our reactions to last night. Fifteen customers all at once is too many, they said. We should have started in January when trade is very slack. Six is a good number to get broken in on. They looked at our crevices and said we should use more cream tonight. I didn't say I never used any! I must admit it feels uncomfortably warm and tingly down there.

We went out again with Geraldine this afternoon; it was good to get fresh air into our lungs. We dress rather drably and are not much troubled by gentlemen. She even saw a customer, who did not recognize her. (We, of course, never recognize them outside the Maison d'Or.)

I told her the conclusions I had reached – about the need to avoid sexual excitement of any kind with my customers. She said I mustn't let what the other girls say influence me like that. It was wrong either way – to go looking for sexual pleasure or to avoid

175

it. 'If it happens, it happens,' she said. 'If not, you just do the best job you can on whoever is your man of the moment.'

'How many give you a *little* thrill?' Ouné asked.

'Most of them. I told you. I like men.'

'And a bigger thrill? *Une petite tresaillement?*'

She shrugged. 'Two or three in every ten.'

'And a real earthquake of a climax?' I asked.

'Not more than two or three times a week.' She chuckled. 'And don't you dare tell the other girls that or I'll scratch your eyes out! Funnily enough, that's the same whether I'm doing fifteen a night or five. That's what I was trying to explain. It's nothing to do with *them*. It's something here inside of *me* that decides when to let me enjoy it.'

Perhaps she is right. Perhaps I will reach that equilibrium in time. But for the moment I feel I must take my own path: eliminate all sexual pleasure and then allow back just as much as I need – not what all those accidental cocks and tools and pricks and weapons accidentally give me.

'I'll tell you one thing,' I said, changing the subject. 'The poverty of most men's imaginations! I mean, they seem to know about six different things to do with a girl – and the moment they see you naked they get so excited they forget four of them.'

Geraldine laughed and agreed.

'It's going to get very boring,' I added. 'Isn't it part of our business to suggest something new to them?'

She looked dubious. 'I wouldn't say it's necessarily boring. Have you ever been rodded at an absolutely rock-steady pace for a long long time? And doesn't it let you build up to the most fantastic *plaisir?*'

Ouné and I exchanged glances and grinned. 'Yes.'

She stared at each of us in turn and said, 'I see! Well, you can treat it like that – on a different time-scale, of course. But over an evening of nearly identical sessions you can build yourself up.' Ouné nodded. 'On the other hand,' Geraldine went on, 'if you actually want some variety and they're not giving it you, there's no harm in making a suggestion to the right man. If it's someone you know quite well and you think he might appreciate it. Of course, you don't simply say, "Here, try this. You'll like it." But you could say, "I'll tell you something one of the other girls told me, and I've never done it that way, but it sounds delicious – let's try it?" Even the most cliché thing ever. You can't go wrong by pretending to be innocent – it's what they look for in a *poulette*.'

'Does the house ever arrange orgies?' Ouné asked.

'Never! Not any of the *maisons de poulettes*. Another of the Countess's rules. Very young girls in this business need to give simple, pure, natural sexual services to sober, reliable men. That's why we have no alcohol on the premises, too. Nothing to inflame us, you see? They had terrible trouble in the old days – screaming hysterics, riots, suicides – with liquor and orgies and unnatural acts all the time. And she's right. You young girls need that simplicity. The most we're allowed to offer our clients is *à deux*. At Christmas, a favoured customer who visits regularly could ask for three. But normally two's the limit.'

'Does that often happen?' I asked. 'Two at a time?'

'It happened twice last night. You must have been upstairs working, both times.'

I laughed. 'That's easy to guess! I think I was only in the salon half an hour all told last night. I didn't dare offer any man less than his full thirty minutes, not after what Mme Dutourd said. Oh, she is an ogress!'

'Ach – she's not so bad. If you keep it between twenty minutes and thirty, she won't grumble. And when we're busy – she'll bless you for using those same tricks to get them off quick!' She checked the clock again. 'And we'll be busy again tonight, I can assure you. Listen! Can't you feel it?'

'What?'

She smiled, more to herself than us. 'Spring! Look about you – all these men, hurrying here, scurrying there. And the vernal sap rising in them like champagne, with this warmth and the lightness in the air. Can't you hear that quiet desperation building up in them! That feverish, melting pressure which keeps them half-stiff for hours, whining at them – get me a girl, must have a girl! Just think of that when you see them wandering into the salon tonight, looking half-drugged with their lust – think of the demiurge that has whipped them to our beds. Think how much we can help them – what relief we can bring. Poor men! Ah, indeed, the poor men!'

Thursday, May 6th.

I thought last night would be a repeat performance of the first, but there was a subtle difference. My first night, after the fourth or fifth customer, I didn't want to look at the men any more. I just wanted to let them poke me as pleasantly as possible, take more than twenty and less than thirty minutes about it, and then go. In fact, there was one man who asked me to pull my chemise up over my eyes – he didn't want me to look at him; and I was happy to oblige.

But last night I found myself observing them, all of them, quite closely. Because of this, I think, I had much less trouble with my own sexual feelings – which made me very glad. One or two moments of slight pleasure – and by no means with the handsomest or most skilled of them, either – otherwise it

178

was acting, acting all the way. And very good, too, though I say so myself. If I were a man, I would be proud to give my love such shattering ecstasies as I spread before them.

While I lay there, with those men pounding away inside me, I kept thinking of Mme Dutourd. *If only she could see me now,* I thought. It was really her I was working to please.

I have had such superb lovers in the past – especially the Duke and Nero Bey, whose sexuality was in every nerve and muscle, every square millimetre of their skin. I once made Nero come just by sucking his toe. I thought something of that must be true of all men, but it is not so. Most of them keep it all in their pricks. I did only fourteen customers last night. Five of them did not even bother to undress. They either bent me over the bed or the back of the chaise longue, or they laid me on the edge of the mattress with my ankles up on their shoulders. And there, in full evening dress, straight from the theatre, they stuck the pride of their flesh into me and screwed away as if I wasn't there. One even went on smoking his cigar! (And dropped hot ash on me, which made me cry out, and cost him a five-franc tip into the bargain.) The look of intense concentration on their faces is most strange when the emotion is not shared.

May 7th.
I am getting lazy in keeping up this diary. I should have said more about my other customers in yesterday's entry. And now I find I have forgotten them already! I did nineteen last night – getting in training for the even heavier traffic my poor *crevasse* must endure tomorrow and Sunday night. The unchanging

179

ritual of our brief encounters is beginning to take on a comforting familiarity; I think my grandmother is wise indeed to limit the services we may offer these men. We *are* very young girls. Our customers are mostly important men with authority and power; and yet here, supported by those rules of hers, we can be their equals, because we, too, are professionals now. There is something very flattering to a girl when an army captain or the head of a large business house comes here and takes an interest in her; and though he buys her *cul,* he is nonetheless a slave to it for a season. And her *cul* is the victor in the end. She subdues him, keeps his money, and goes on to another conquest. He creeps home with (to coin a phrase) his tail between his legs.

And that ritual is our chief support – or our most immediate support, anyway. We return to the salon after each session in our rooms, our eyes are bright, our lips wet and parted, and we look as if our last encounter merely whetted our craving for a real man. Our eyes are keen and predatory until we meet our next mark; then we lower them modestly. We blush. Our nearly naked bosoms heave. We have found him at last and the excitement is almost too much for our girlish bodies to bear. He approaches and says something. We sit down on his lap. His hands relish their delicious freedom to stray in and out of our chemises, caressing our breasts, feeling our nipples, testing the moisture down in our *crevasses.* Our breathing grows disordered. He races us upstairs. The swaying of our generous hips and *derrières* brings him to the boil as he enters our room. If he looks into our eyes, he sees us melting with desire.

And there the atmosphere changes subtly. We are private, alone, secret. We look at his tool, assess its length and girth and plan ways of limiting its freedom

180

if either is too large – but always we are surprised and delighted to see it there, so manly, true, and bold. Then we lie so, stand so, bend so ... we cry out in delight, we moan, we shiver, we sigh ... We remember what *plaisirs* were like and we recreate their image to perfection now. And all the while we gauge his performance to a T, matching our rising ecstasy to his, so that we both explode together. Then we pet him and pamper him and beg he will come and enjoy us again (and privately hope we will be able to recognize him when he does!). Then we return to the salon, bright-eyed, wet lips parted, looking as if our last encounter had merely whetted our craving for a real man. Our eyes are once again keen and predatory ...

Monday, May 10th.
I could not write a word all weekend. What a time we had of it! Between Saturday noon and this morning at 3 a.m., 447 gentlemen paid nearly 3,200 francs for the pleasure of standing in line to take one of us nine sweet, innocent young *poulettes* up to our rooms and screw our tails off. I did exactly fifty, twenty-seven on Saturday, the rest on Sunday. To-night it is raining heavily and even stern old Mme Dutourd is glad we shall be almost empty. We are 'only' expecting about fifty gentlemen to call, all told. Half a dozen each. I hope none of them is expecting too much from me after that Marathon of venery.

In the end it got almost comical – the kind of comedy that is close to hysteria. It was literally quickies only. Ten minutes each, and any trick we knew to get them off quickly – and, as Geraldine had said, no harsh words from madame. I discovered muscles in my *canal* that would astonish the professors of anatomy at the Sorbonne.

The Saturday and Sunday crowds are quite different from the weekday ones. All our stolid *bourgeois* customers – the lawyers and doctors and captains of industry – are in the bosoms of their family. I remember now, while I think of it, a lawyer asked me last Thursday night how many times a week I thought he ought to roger his wife, who was twenty-four. He asked *me!* While I was fishing to discover what sort of answer he was hoping to hear, he said, 'I think once a week, don't you? I give her a jolly good rogering every Saturday. Twice when we go to bed and once in the morning before we get up and go to church. I think that ought to keep her happy, eh?'

I was reminded of her yesterday when I heard the church bells ringing: I thought of her sitting there in her pew with her *centre de délices* still tingling from

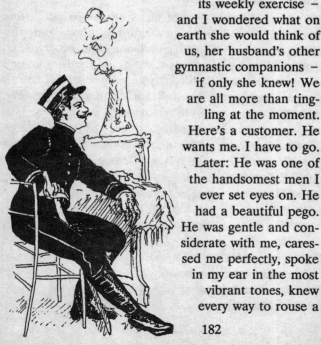

its weekly exercise – and I wondered what on earth she would think of us, her husband's other gymnastic companions – if only she knew! We are all more than tingling at the moment. Here's a customer. He wants me. I have to go. Later: He was one of the handsomest men I ever set eyes on. He had a beautiful pego. He was gentle and considerate with me, caressed me perfectly, spoke in my ear in the most vibrant tones, knew every way to rouse a

182

woman to pleasure ... and every morsel of mine was fake! I have triumphed at last. Another week of that perfect control and I can start to build on it.

I was about to describe our weekend crowd. They are mostly young officers and students who have saved up for us. A jolly, tolerant, amused, and amusing bunch – which made the work tolerable. We sang for them, danced with them, and took them above, two at a time often enough. Last night, when the doors had closed and there were still more than twenty waiting their turn, Mme Dutourd let me take three gay young cadets up at once; and I just lay there, half asleep, while they leaped on and off me in turns, laughing and joking all the time; and it was only twenty minutes for all three of them. They'd never have taken as little as seven minutes each.

In the two days I earned 175 francs in fees and 50 in tips. No one expects the students to tip, except a few rich ones – but they mostly like to flatter themselves with girls in the dearer aristocratic houses.

Next Saturday and Sunday will be much quieter. The annual spring manoeuvres begin next week.

Wednesday, May 12th. D'Alembert returned for his usual Tuesday night exercise last night.

Again things were very quiet on account of the rain. I told him he could take an hour with me if he liked and we lay there quite a while just talking before he enjoyed me. He wanted to know all my thoughts and feelings and I enjoyed unburdening myself to him. But I'm sorry to say I had quite a *plaisir* with him later. It hit me completely out of the blue. So I'm not in as much control of my desired as I like to think. Still, if it had to be with somebody, I'm glad it was him. I've grown quite fond of him now.

Friday 14th.

I am absolutely shattered. Mme Dutourd called me into her parlour this morning and said if I did not put a bit more life and warmth into my work, she would have to kick me out. I began at once to shiver like a jelly. I could not believe it. I have been faking such marvellous ecstasies for my clients, I'm sure all of them were deceived. But it seems that is not enough. They say I am remote. Do not talk to them, ask their names, chatter with them – tell them what wonderful bodies and massive tools they have. I could not believe my ears. Also the shame! How could I face my grandmother if this happened to me?

I swallowed my pride and cried a little ... said how sorry I was and would really try better in future ... et cetera.

Tonight I shall go back to the old way – try and find a bit of genuine sexual pleasure with each and every customer.

Saturday, May 15th.

I may be too exhausted to complete this, but I must try while it is still fresh in my mind – and oh, what a pleasant exhaustion it is, too!

184

Not that last evening, Friday, started at all pleasantly. The Spring Fever seems to be abating in this much cooler, showery weather and we are back to our more normal traffic – even less with almost all the military away. I only did six customers last night, so I was really able to concentrate on them and give them all a nice long, relaxed time upstairs with me – and I could talk to them first, down in the salon ... and so put them in a pleasant, easy mood for their adventure above.

And I did everything I knew to please them – wriggled, giggled, squirmed, sighed, rubbed my body all over them, offered them new and exciting poses ... And if we aren't allowed to suck their creamsticks, we can get very close to it, I find, with a gentle kiss down there and some work with our nimble fingers and soft cream. No one told me kissing is forbidden and I'm not going to ask. I heard no complaints from the customers, anyway.

And a complaint is something I went out of my way to get. While each of my six gentleman lay there, getting back his breath, I asked him if he had enjoyed me. Of course, they always answer yes to that, but I pressed the question. I told them I was very new to the work and therefore most eager to please my lovers. So if there was anything, any tiny little thing, where they would have preferred me to do something a bit different, please, please say so. One of them said he didn't like it when I lay a bit sideways on to him, making his ramrod go at a slight diagonal into me; another said he wished I'd used that little footstool to lift my *derrière* higher for him (I keep forgetting that bit of furniture!) – and so on. But they were all very minor suggestions and they assured me over and over that I was one of the best *poulettes* they'd ever enjoyed.

The trouble was that in straining to please *them* so mightily, I came desperately near to orgasm with each single one of them. Near – but I never actually reached it. And that's the most terrible thing of all, in my view. The tension within me by the time madame said the last goodnight and locked the doors was unbearable. I looked enviously at Ouné who was going upstairs with her latest all-night customer – she gets them nearly every night now. The word is spreading. When she had gone, Geraldine said to me, 'I was so afraid my last gentleman was going to change his mind and stay all night. I think I'd have screamed.' There were four or five other girls there, all of whom agreed. Eight hours of unbroken sleep, especially after a nice quiet night like this, was all we and our overworked *concons* desired.

I have to include all that to explain why I behaved as I did. Half an hour after the house fell to silence, Hortense, one of the maids, came tiptoe into my room with a light. I don't know why she chose me. Perhaps Eros himself guided her steps. Anyway, she told me two young cadets, one of whom had been here last Saturday, had broken out of barracks and brought themselves back for more. They'd tried to break in through her bedroom window, which is in the basement, and now they were threatening to kick up such a stink if they weren't satisfied. 'Which other girl shall I rouse?' she asked.

From the way they had behaved, I wouldn't have wished it on any of them. 'I'll come and talk to these two,' I said, meaning to persuade them into leaving sensibly and returning at the proper hour. But the moment I glimpsed them through the slightly open door, a completely different plan occurred to me. I withdrew at once into the passage outside the salon and explained it in whispers to Hortense.

I would do both of them, I said, but in such a way they would think they were getting two different girls. I didn't know which of them was our previous customer but neither was among the cadets I had done last weekend – at least I did not think so. She was to tell them that all the girls had all-night lovers. (We always call our customers 'lovers' in front of other customers.) But two of them were with fat, boring old grandfathers who just lay there and snored; they'd both be overjoyed to slip away and have a bit of real fun in bed with two such gorgeous specimens of young manhood. 'Say it will take some time to organize ... make out you're doing them an enormous favour ... they may have to wait a bit before their girl can slip away. Or they may be lucky and enjoy her at once. That's the only way it can be done. But promise them they'll each get three goes with a pretty young *poulette* before morning.'

She stared at me in admiration, and warned, 'One of them has never been with a woman in his life – the fair one, Victor. The other is called Paul – he's been here before, as I said. Where shall I put them? They can't wait down here.'

'No.' I was thinking furiously. 'Those spare rooms – are they still ready?'

She nodded. 'Lucky they're so close to your room!'

'Yes. Put the virgin opposite Ouné's. Victor, you said? And Paul in the one beyond. While you're explaining it all down here, I'll run upstairs and make sure both rooms are absolutely ready. And I'll also leave them some interesting literature and pictures to look at. Then I'll go and wait in my own room. Come and tell me when they're ready for me.'

As I lit the two spare rooms, I wondered why I had made this decision – so suddenly and so completely. I think it was the sight of the two of them, both at once and side by side, that did it: handsome young men in their very early twenties, looking really splendid in their uniforms. I remembered Geraldine's words about the intolerable pressures that build up in men – and it occurred to me that, thanks to my evening's efforts, I myself was now in precisely the same condition. And suddenly it was not two customers waiting in there, nor even two gorgeous young men, it was a double-barrelled battery of male sexual power sent to relieve me. Relief *columns!* Is it not the function of the military to provide such things to civilians in distress?

I waited in my room, in a strangely excited state, and heard them go past in an orgy of hushes and creaking floorboards. Moments later, Hortense came to tell me they were all ready, eager, and panting. 'No argument at all,' she said. 'You're a marvel, Mam'selle Jenny.'

Feeling like a kind of virgin myself – certainly I was trembling – I crossed the passage to the room opposite Ouné's, where Victor was no doubt waiting in an absolute lather.

He was! I never saw a man so agitated. 'Mam'selle …' he blurted out at soon as I had introduced myself (as 'Jeannette'). I put my finger to my lips to remind him to whisper. 'I really think this is a most terrible mistake. It was Paul who …'

I walked directly to him, taking him by surprise; I draped my arms around his neck, raised my lips to his, and silenced him with a long, warm kiss. 'You tease!' I whispered as we broke. 'Surely you could never do a thing like that? Come in here – get a poor young girl all excited just to look at you – and then go away without putting her out of her misery?'

Truth to tell, I *was* quite excited by now. But so was he. And here is one unavoidable difference between a man and a woman: A virgin girl in the arms of a skilled lover could be taken on a two-hour tour of wonderland before their first pleasuring is done; a virgin man, too excited for his own good, cannot make that same journey, no matter how skilled the female pilot of his craft.

I had hoped to show Victor so much of the thrills a man and a woman may enjoy together before that ultimate delight takes them in its grip; but I could see there was no point in even trying. Indeed, if I wasn't careful, he was going to finish it all in his trousers. Fleur told me that happened to her once with a virgin – he just touched her breast and filled his underpants with the stuff.

'D'you know what I really, really, really enjoy?' I asked him, all breathless.

'What?'

'A quick, rough go first, just to relax all my body, and then, half an hour later, perhaps, a nice, long, gentle, relaxed poke. Oh, Victor, I'd love you forever if you did that to me.'

I didn't even want to touch his pego yet, for fear it might explode. I just drew up my chemise behind, bent over the back of the gilded chair, and murmured, 'Please? Oh please be quick! I'm just dying for the feel of you inside me there.'

It was not as bad with him as I had feared. He actually managed half a dozen thrusts before he spent in me. And, as always when they're as swift as that, he didn't leave much of a deposit behind.

'I've done it!' he said in wonder. 'At last I really have done it!'

'You've got rid of the fever,' I told him. 'Now your temperature's closer to normal we can really linger over it ...'

'Was it nice for you, too?' he asked.

I caressed his knob, which at once leaped into life again. 'It was a very tasty hors d'oeuvre, my sweet Victor. I'll be back in a while for the real feast.'

Now for Paul. He was in the room beyond Ouné's. As I went in I thought, *I've got to be a different person.* I don't know why. All I really needed to do was give them different names and go on being me underneath; but I just felt this conviction I had to be a different person, too. I borrowed Jacqui's movements, which are languorous and slow, and Ouné's manner, with her heavy-lidded eyes and that permanent slight smile, which suggests some ultimate naughtiness before the act, unreachable pleasure during it, and delicious memories afterwards.

He was already undressed and in the bed, looking at some stereoscopes. I went over and sat on its edge. I told him I was 'Célestine' and I'd just had the most boring poke ever from a poor little clerk with a tool no bigger than a crayon.

'How about that then!' He threw back the sheets and waved it at me – and it was indeed, magnificent – a relief *column* of no uncertain magnitude! My eyes spoke for me.

'Oh, M Paul, you've no idea how we girls long to see something like that – and how rare a sight it is, even in a place like this. Oh, I want to feel that inside me very soon.'

'I say! Really?' He stared at it as if it might have changed since the last time he looked at it.

'Yes, quick! I can't leave my little clerk too long. You know I'm breaking the strictest rule in the house for you? But if I find him still asleep when I get back, I'll stay much longer next time.'

The promise, and my sultry way of delivering it, delighted him. 'In that case, mam'selle,' he asked, 'please tell me what is your favourite position?'

I looked at him as if lost in amazement. 'I can hardly believe it,' I whispered. 'D'you know – not one man in a hundred who visits this house cares a scrap for the pleasure of us poor girls. Ah, but do you really mean it?'

'Of course,' he replied with diffident modesty.

'In that case ... oh, m'sieu, how kind you are! If you will screw me in my favourite position, then I will do anything you want when I return next time.'

'Anything?'

'Within the rules of the Maison d'Or, you understand. I've taken enough risk already for the sake of enjoying you ...'

All this while I was sprinkling cushions about the floor. Then, in the middle of them, I placed the little arched footstool that is in every room here, and, letting my chemise drift from my shoulders, I lay fully naked except for my silk stockings, face down on the carpet with the stool beneath my tummy and hips, where it lifted my little *derrière* invitingly for him. This seems to be the most powerfully erotic position in which a women can offer her body to a man; it makes her look so vulnerable, so accessible, so demurely *ready*.

Actually, my *derrière* is not so little these days; I have grown into quite a woman. 'Invitingly full and deliciously soft' would be more apt. Anyway, Paul could not believe his luck as he stood between my spreadeagled feet. 'And you just want me to go straight in? Now?'

'Yes! Yes!' I squirmed in a fever of desire.

He knelt between my thighs and rubbed his knob up and down my crevice, picking up some of my juices. I gave a sigh of joy at the touch of him. Then he leaned forward, lay upon me, and went straight in. 'What sort of ... pace d'you like?' he asked.

'Strong!' I moaned. 'Lusty. Deep and hard. Hard as you can. Oh, *feed* it to me!'

He went at me all he was worth. I was not reaching for my climax yet. All I wanted was to clear away those earlier tensions, get myself utterly relaxed. My next session with him would be the one that would really set me flying.

Oh, but he was good! He almost upset my own idea of the right pacing. 'Now!' I whimpered. 'Slowly! Long and slow and gentle.'

He obeyed. It *was* pleasant, too; but those muscles and nerves that were grasping for the other rhythm were thwarted, and the danger passed.

I gave out little cries of surprise and began squeezing my *canal* in time with them. 'I'm going to spend!' he warned desperately.

'Yeeees!' I sighed in the final transports of ecstasy.

And as his magnificent weapon exploded and throbbed within me, I performed a mighty *plaisir* to keep him company. I will not say I faked it, rather that it was an embellishment of my actual state at that moment – a promissory note, redeemable in about an hour's time. Anyway, I was very happy.

Or, rather, the Jacqui-Ouné girl inside me was. I felt sure that 'her' partial possession of me had something to do with my changed condition. As I returned to Victor I thought I would give 'Jeannette' a little more character this time. Before, she had been nervous, scared of breaking the rules; now she'd be insouciant, slightly giddy, devil-may-care.

Victor was actually asleep when I returned to his room! But he woke when I slipped between the sheets. 'Now!' I cuddled up beside him. 'Take all the time you want, my darling. Do all those things you've only ever dreamed of doing. This warm young body beside you is absolutely, utterly yours.'

He was diffident at the outset, until I suggested things to do: 'Put your hand right over my breast – yes! Caress it like that. Squeeze my nipples very gently. Oooh, yes! D'you feel how they harden? That's my enjoyment beginning ...' And so I guided him through all the pleasure gardens in the entire citadel of the female body.

'Would you like to look at me now?' I suggested. 'You know where I mean? Down there.'

I pushed off the sheets, drew up my knees, and spread my thighs wide. He went down and played around with me, using his fingers for a while. This time I guided him with little sighs and *ohs* of delight.

'You want to kiss it, don't you,' I said. 'Go on.'

He was drugged now with the rising of his longing. It drove out the last vestige of his shyness; he just drifted in the grip of instincts too ancient to number.

'D'you want to know something that will really drive a girl wild with desire?' I asked, all innocence. His eyes almost melted with longing at my words. 'See that little rosebud of flesh at the top of the folds – where the two inner lips begin? Put *your* lips around that and play on it with your tongue ... aaaah – yes! Yes ... yes ... yes ... *Mon dieu!* You are so marvellous!'

'Could you ...' he gasped, 'do that to me, too?'

I swear I forgot the rule. It was so long (well, almost a month) since I'd had that wonderful sensation of living, virile gristle in my mouth that I could not resist the invitation. 'We can both do it at the same time,' I said.

We were at it for a good twenty minutes. A *good* twenty minutes? A *wonderful* twenty minutes! We had *soixante-neuf* side by side, then with me on top, then with him on top – my favourite, because there's always that fear he'll forget himself and push hard. That edge of danger never fails to excite me.

'I don't think I can stay out of you any longer,' he gasped at length, holding me off him.

'You're marvellous,' I told him once again – and I meant it. 'Most men stop much too soon for me.'

We lay in each other's arms for a minute, savouring the approaching moment of his going in. 'I had intended to show you every possible position,' I murmured. 'But we've gone beyond that, my darling. I'm enjoying your marvellous body too much to turn myself back into teacher. I just want to lie here and ride those waves of ecstasy with you. D'you mind?'

'Do I mind!' He choked on the thought. 'I just want to lie on top of you and ... would that be too dull?'

I couldn't wait. I half pulled him up there, half wriggled myself beneath him. I don't know how many dozen men have lain on me in exactly that position this past ... God! Have I been here only eleven days? Anyway, none of them was like that. Somehow I had become a girl with her lover again – not a *poulette* having a lucky experience, just a loving girl. I don't know what we did. We simply waltzed away together in that old thoughtless delirium. We had a genuine climax, simultaneously, of a kind I hadn't known since leaving Nero.

Victor fell asleep at once. I rose, feeling on top of the world again, and, having douched and made myself sweet once more, merely clutched my chemise about me as I dashed up the passage to Paul.

He heard me coming and I had the thrill of seeing his lollipop grow hard and hot in anticipation of our joy. And it needed to be. I was still on the plateau where Victor had left me. Paul hardly got his head between my thighs before I was away again, on surges and ripples of pleasure. He couldn't believe it. He thought I was faking. But there was no arguing against the strawberry blushes on my skin.

194

'I don't know what's happened to me tonight, Paul,' I told him. 'It's just that you were so sweet and thoughtful to me before, I suppose. That always softens our hearts, you know. And you're such a marvellous lover, I don't mind what you do to me now. Just keep it going. Have me in any position you like – every position you ever dreamed of enjoying a girl! But keep it up.'

Dawn was over the rooftops before *he* finally gave in and spent; by then I had lost count.

As I left to go back to my 'clerk,' he murmured, 'That maid – Hortense?'

'Yes?'

'She promised us three goes. Don't come back. I think I just had thirty-three.'

I snatched what sleep I could. At eleven, I went to Victor and sucked him off and then did the same for Paul. When I make a promise, I honour it! I didn't even tell them to keep it a secret. If I'm dismissed, I'm dismissed. I no longer care much about that.

Good heavens! That's the whole of Saturday afternoon gone in writing this. I've half an hour in which to get ready for this evening's encounters. And yet I feel that in some curious way I am ready now – more ready for my customers than at any time since I came here. I don't know what difference last night's adventures have made. If anything, that powerful reminder of what real sexual love is like ought to leave me more dispirited than ever – and yet it seems to have done the opposite.

Sunday, 16th May.

It's a fine, sunny day and I've come out here in the Bois to write this, sitting with Ouné and Geraldine in the shade of the trees. I can actually see my villa

195

from here! How I long to point it out to Ouné. She saw it, of course, when we came back last month – but from the other side. I'm sure she hasn't recognized it. But with Geraldine here I dare not even hint at it. Geraldine – I make you a silent promise here and now: When my secret must come out, you shall be the first to know.

So, was I right? Is everything changed? I say a resounding yes! I actually *enjoyed* every customer I had last night! I don't mean I enjoyed them as I enjoyed Victor and Paul – not at all. I entertained nine men in my bed last night and never got within a thousand miles of even one small *plaisir*. And yet I thoroughly enjoyed them all. I enjoyed the work – *as work*. The pleasure they took in me was like a warm bath to my soul. Their kindness and their gratitude almost overwhelmed me. I felt appreciated, wanted, needed, useful. I feel *good!*

I've been trying to think of some parallel in other trades. I suppose if a woman nurses her own husband back to health, that's one sort of pleasure. And if she's paid to nurse a sick stranger – same illness, same nursing, same recovery ... it wouldn't be the same pleasure, but it would be a pleasure nonetheless, surely? And if she nursed the stranger *as if* he were her husband – i.e., going well beyond the strict requirements of the commercial arrangement between them – then her pleasure might even be greater in some particular ways. What might be thought mere duty to her husband would be noble altruism to the stranger ... and so on.

That's the nearest I can get to it. Somehow, what happened between me (that is, Jeannette-Célestine) and those two cadets has enabled me to go beyond the strict requirements of my commercial relationship with my customers and 'nurse' their sexual lust (a kind of sickness, maybe?) *as if* it were my own true love's. When they have finished in me, my *vagin* feels good. It is not the feeling of orgasm, just the good feeling of a job well done. But why concentrate on my *vagin?* The whole of my body feels good.

I don't think that is at all what my grandmother used to feel. She is like Ouné, a being who lives for sexual fulfilment and cannot see any need to distinguish its sources. I am more like Geraldine. I can take fire when the mood and the man are right. If not, well, I still do not disappoint.

This reminds me of a conversation I once had with the Duke. We were talking about Carlos's attempts to make me a prostitute, and I said the worst thing about the trade must be having to open yourself to the most awful creatures, the deformed, the hideously ugly, the maimed ... And the Duke said, 'No. The worst of it is when you don't even care whether the next man who undresses you is Quasimodo or Adonis himself – when they are all one and the same to you. That must be the end.'

I thought that very profound at the time but now I can see he missed the point. *I* don't care if the next man who undresses me is Quasimodo – but not because I have become so indifferent to them all that I just don't care. Quite the opposite – I *do* care. I care for Quasimodo's hunger as much as for anyone else's, and I could do the same good work for him as for all the rest, and take the same pride in it, too. If not more. I don't suppose the Duke will ever understand that, especially of me.

One other thing – Lord, look at the time! We must start returning to the Maison d'Or soon – and I say it with a lilt in my heart now, not that old sinking feeling. Anyway, I must get this down: Captain

Hubert – the monocled man who made Ouné's first time so uncomfortable – came back last night and made a beeline for me. Of course I was full of trepidation when he made me lie on the carpet with the little arched footstool under me. Looking at his weapon, I didn't think it as long as Ouné had said, but it still looked formidable. However, as he probed away, going deeper each time ... waiting for me to wince, I realized I was more than equal to him now!

I let him ram to the very hilt, which did just put the slightest pressure on the throat of my *canal*. I gave out a pretend bellow of pain. 'Why didn't you say something sooner?' he asked angrily.

I thought of telling him I was one of those weird girls who like a *bit* of pain, but then I realized I could convey the thought more subtly. So I said I didn't want to show him how inadequate I was.

'Well where does it start hurting?' he asked, beginning to probe me again, millimetre by millimetre.

'There!' I said – wincing to prove it – when he still had about an inch to feed me. And I gave my *concon* a squeeze to make him feel he'd touched something. 'No, don't stop!' I added urgently – before he could demonstrate he had no intention of stopping.

'What d'you mean?' He kept on prodding away.

'Ouch! No – go on! Aiee, that hurt! Do it again!'

'What nonsense is this?' he cried, ramming to the full, but harmless, depth of him. I collapsed in an apparent climax of pain-pleasure. So then he went on ramming away to full depth until he also spent; all that while I gave muffled screams into the pillows and almost fainted with rapture. It was a very puzzled, bewildered officer who said he'd call again soon! I'll have him so confused, he won't know whether he's coming or going. Perhaps then he'll stop doing both.

Weds. 19th May.

D'Alembert again chose me last night. Very loving and gentle. The usual thing happened – a genuine *plaisir* for me, my first since Victor and Paul. And since *them* I have lain with 37 other gentlemen. So why d'Alembert? He is no different from them – or so I thought, until he started telling me how I have begun to haunt him. He wants to call here every day, lives in a feverish state of semi-erection just thinking about me ... and so on. The last thing a girl in my position needs.

I told him on pain of death not to reveal it but I would be leaving the Maison d'Or early next month.

'I feared something of that sort,' he said. 'You are not like the other *poulettes*. You are ... unique. You are moving on to one of the aristocratic houses, yes?'

'Never! I am leaving the entire business, in a way.'

'Aha! To be someone's mistress! Who is he? No, never mind. But how much is he paying you? I'll double it – I don't care what it is. I don't know if I can afford it, but I do know what I can *not* afford – and that would be to lose you ...'

After a lot more conversation in that vein, I asked if it really meant so much to him.

'It is my life,' he replied.

'Then I shall not let you die, have no fear.'

'What do you mean?'

'Be patient. My body seems to have taken a liking to you, as well. I will let you know what she decides. Now tell me about the other girls here. How am I "different"?' And I went on to explain what Mme Dutourd had threatened.

He was aghast. I think he would have rushed out, hired a sword, and run her through if I had not detained him. 'There is no comparison between you and them,' he blustered. 'Those other trollops. This must be pure jealousy. Some of the other girls have poured poison in her ear.'

'Have you lain with them all?' I asked.

'From time to time, before you came, yes.'

His descriptions startled me. It shows our clients are more aware of our true feelings than we suppose; their actual spending is genuine enough – after all, the evidence that runs out of us afterwards is not something a man can easily fake! But they are not above faking in other ways. Are we all in one giant conspiracy here? This much I remember of his words:

Jacqui has no idea what a climax is. She has seen mares being led to stud and that is what she imitates for the benefit of her customers. I would do her a favour to bring her on a twosome with me to show her something more human.

Yvette is careless. She lies there giving out a sigh every three seconds and thinking about some dress or hat she'd like to buy; but sometimes her carelessness lets her down and a cunning man can get under her pleasure and lift her to the skies before she realizes what's happening.

No one could ever do that with Blanche and Arlette; but a clever man will choose the pair of them together. They can light fires in each other and they can't help warming him if he gets into the furnace at the right moment.

Franchine and Geraldine, though so different physically, are very alike with men. You know you have anything up to twenty-seven-and-a-half minutes of truly caring attention from them; after that it gets a trifle brittle and they'll hurry you on. Geraldine is better at it than Franchine, but only because she's more experienced. Kindness and sympathy is what lights fires in them; a skilled man can nearly always trick them into the real thing.

Fleur is shy about her tiny breasts. She compensates by making all her other excitements even more appetizing. She has the best lingerie of any of the girls, and she knows more ways of flaunting her body than any *poulette* he ever knew. A man can do two things with her – either accept all this bounty as it is offered, or pay such extravagant attention to her breasts that she is overcome with delight and gratitude. That's how you make her lose control.

'And Ouné?' I asked.

He shrugged. 'Since you arrived. mam'selle …'

I told him he would do me the greatest favour if he tried her out for me. 'So really,' I summarized, 'you see your business here as tricking us poor working girls into genuine pleasure with you.'

'Isn't that what the battle's always been about?'

'But why do you care about our pleasure at all? It's yours you've paid for, not ours.'

'But your pleasure is mine as well. Otherwise I could simply screw a lump of warm meat.'

The image was so brutal, I wished I had not asked.

Friday, 21st May.

D'Alembert came again tonight and chose Ouné. He could not look me in the eye on his way out. I suppose I shall hear his report on Tuesday.

I have just done the Prefect of Police, M de Paty. I knew he was someone important by the looks of envy from the other girls. I cannot understand this obsession they have with the social status of our customers. No doubt they imagined me being carried away on waves of ecstasy with him, but when his clothes were off him he was a man like any other. He was well satisfied when he left, I think – and that was my only joy in the transaction.

Sunday, 23rd May.

A strange thing happened yesterday afternoon. The manoeuvres had ended and we were ready for utter pandemonium. Our regulars had been warned off, and we girls were all available for service in the salon at two. And just as well, for I never saw such a randy crowd of young officers before – fit, healthy, vigorous men in the prime of their lives and with two weeks' pent-up lust to slake. It was a day to heed Geraldine's advice: 'If it happens, let it.'

The electric crackle of their sexual excitement was infectious. I could feel it among all the girls as we perfumed and powdered ourselves before the doors were opened; I don't care what they claim to feel or not to feel, the prospects for this afternoon and evening were highly pleasurable to us all. You only had to look at us to feel it.

I took three upstairs in the first thirty-five minutes – and 'let it happen' with them all. After that I steadied down a bit and concentrated on their pleasure, instead. Very few of them left the Maison d'Or, I noticed. I asked Geraldine why, and she said it was always like that after manoeuvres. They'd get one shot out of their locker early, then hang around in the exciting atmosphere provided by nine girls – young, pretty, scantily clad, and available – and, after recharging their cannon for a few hours, pick another partner and go upstairs with her to 'fire the big one.'

Around four, when there was a bit of a lull, we were allowed a fifteen-minute break, two at a time, in the boudoir, for a coffee and some light snacks.

Ouné and I took our break together. We had barely seated ourselves when little Jacqui came staggering in looking so sick I thought she would pass out.

'What is it?' we asked. 'What has he *done* to you?' (Interesting that that was our common thought!)

'I think I've been poisoned,' she gasped, putting her hand to her stomach. 'It was ever such a ... ooooh!' She flopped down on the sofa, shivering and still fighting to breathe. None of her clothing needed loosening; all I could think of to do was feel her brow and test her pulse. Her temperature seemed normal enough, but her heart was racing like mad.

'Open your eyes,' Ouné told her. She suspected laudanum but Jacqui's pupils were normal.

'Did he give you anything strange to smoke?' I asked. 'Tell us how it happened. Who was it?'

She was somewhat calmer now, reassured by our company and our concern. 'Dumont,' she said, 'the big captain with the waxed moustaches. He was just having his climax, and I was giving out my sighs and things, when suddenly I thought I was going to die. My heart stopped. My whole insides turned over ...'

I began to laugh. They both stared at me in astonishment. 'Jacqui, little darling!' I said. 'Don't you know what that was?'

'What?' It was Ouné who asked the question.

'Can't you guess?' I replied. 'Suppose *you'd* never felt one before and it hit you – a big, strong one – out of the blue ...'

Ouné grinned. 'D'you think so? Could it be?'

'It's exactly what happened to me the first time. I had no idea what had hit me. I thought I was dying.'

'What? What are you talking about?' Jacqui looked at each of us in turn. But I think she already half-guessed, for when we told her she had just 'enjoyed' her first *plaisir d'amour,* she gasped, blushed scarlet, laughed, hid her face in shame, and asked if they were all like that.

We told her. 'And listen, darling,' I added. 'Pay no attention to what those other girls say. They just like to talk big and pretend they're utterly indifferent. We all come with customers now and then – ask Geraldine if you don't believe me. The thing to do is, don't fight against them and don't go looking for them. If they happen, they happen ... *alors!* It's as good as a five-franc tip.'

At three o'clock this morning, when we locked our doors and bade them all good night (no all-nighters allowed since today is another heavy siege for us), Jacqui came to my room and asked shyly if she could sleep the night out with with me; she was too tense to sleep alone, she said.

We were both too tired to talk for long; I had done thirty-six, she thirty-two. I asked her how she felt now, about the day's great discovery. She said it had happened again with her very next customer, and then several times more during the evening.

'How many times is "several"?' I asked.

'Nine,' she whispered in horror. 'I just seemed to stay within reach of it all the time. I could sort of call it into me whenever I wanted. Oh Jenny, what am I going to do? The shame of it!'

I told her it was like a new toy; she'd soon grow tired of playing with it. I added that I had enjoyed at least ten myself that day. 'Sometimes it happens like that. There was so much sex and excitement in the atmosphere down there this evening. I'm sure that's why it hit you when it did. But at other times I can go all week without being stirred in the slightest. Just accept it for what it is and be grateful.'

While I was busy – what a feeble word – two young cadets came into the salon and made utter asses of themselves. They asked for a couple of girls nobody had heard of – Jeannette and Célestine – and said they'd enjoyed them last week. Everyone knew they were lying when they swore those girls had sucked them off. 'How men do love to boast!' Geraldine said when she told me of it.

Wednesday, 26th May.
M d'Alembert came as usual last night and said I should have told him about Ouné before. If I was going to leave, I had passed him on to a most acceptable substitute. Indeed, I noticed she was so acceptable that he didn't even give me a farewell session. O faithless Man – thank God!

Mme Dutourd, in her blackest, thunder-and-lightning mood, called me to her room this afternoon. She began by barking at me: 'Well – do I call you Jenny or Jeannette or Célestine, mam'selle? Or just plain liar and cheat?'

My heart fluttered wildly and my throat went dry. I lowered my eyes and tried desperately to gather my thoughts – already knowing that this was my moment of dismissal. 'If you will just let me explain, madame ...' I began, having no idea what I'd say next – but knowing full well she wouldn't let me get a word in edgwise, anyway.

She sniffed. 'Yes ... well ... perhaps I owe you that much at least.' It was very grudging.

'I did not keep the money I took from those cadets. I invented two extra customers during the rush on Saturday and paid you that way. I cannot prove it, of course, but ...'

'I'm more interested in why you did it,' she said with ominous intonation.

I thought of reminding her how the other girls had been so grateful that no all-nighters had asked for them, but I knew she would never believe me to be so altruistic as that.

I sighed. 'I don't honestly know, madame.'

'That will not do, mam'selle. You must try.'

My eyes met hers, pleading for some little show of pity, or even of understanding. But there was nothing in that granite wall of implacability. So I thought I might as well let her know it straight. 'I hope I don't insult you, then, Mme Dutourd, when I say I do not believe you can know how it feels to walk into a place like this and ... I mean, I had known only seven men in my life before I came here – and I did fifteen on my first day. Can't you understand what an assault that was on my ... the invasion of my ...' I lapsed into silence.

Yet, in some odd way, I felt her hostility had fallen away; not that she was suddenly all warm and friendly, just watchful. 'Go on,' she encouraged.

'What?'

'Tell me how you would have liked me to behave? This is not a trap – I truly wish to know.'

I did not believe her, of course, but I said. 'You could have shown a little sympathy.'

She actually smiled – and not unpleasantly. There was even a hint of sadness in her eyes. 'In your case,' she said, 'I believe I could have. But you are rare ...' She held up a finger to ward off an interruption I had not been going to make. 'I'm coming to that. But just think of what some of those other *poulettes* would make of "sympathy"! It would be a licence to open their legs and fall asleep up there. I've been in this business over twenty years, you know. I've tried every way to make it easy for you young girls to adapt to it – and believe me, I do know how desperately hard it is for you all, especially being in such a stormy, tempestuous time of your own lives.'

As always happens when beastly people relent and are nice to me, I began to go all soft and tearful.

'And *have* you adapted to the work?' she asked.

I nodded and blinked at the water in my eyes.

'And you've managed it in only three weeks! Could you have done it so swiftly on your own? If I hadn't been here, giving you a focus for all your emotional storms and angers. Of course it's a violation of your dignity! Of course it's an invasion of your most private self! Of course it fills you with anger! The question is – who do you take that anger out on? The other girls? The customers? Yourself?' She smiled. 'Or a hard-faced old bitch who hasn't a drop of fellow feeling in her body?'

I was amazed – and full of admiration, too. 'Why don't you tell us these things, madame?'

'No!' she snapped, becoming her old self for a moment. 'And don't you dare do it either. D'you understand me? I'm trusting you – something I have never done before.'

I gulped. 'May *I* now ask why, madame?'

'Because, Mam'selle Jenny, I believe you are wasted in this place. Tell me, have you ever heard of a stable of young fillies' – *pouliches* was her word – 'formerly run by a certain M Vallodon? He passed to his glory – and in a state of no uncertain glory, himself, I may add! – about eighteen months ago?'

I kept a perfectly straight face and said I had not. Was it an aristocratic brothel like the ones owned by our own employers?

'No, it is the next step above that. They are young ladies of extreme beauty and refinement – known as the *crème de la crème*. They have little villas in Sèvres and Ville d'Avray and entertain only two clients a day – one in the afternoon, one in the evening.'

'How dull,' I commented. I was on tenterhooks, feeling sure she knew it all and was just playing me. She said, 'Three hundred francs a day? Is it so dull?'

'They may earn it, Mme Dutourd, but how much are they permitted to keep?'

207

'Eighty percent.' She could not understand my coolness – which was encouraging, for it meant she knew nothing about my true wealth.

Also – I realized somewhat late – *eighty* percent was an interesting answer; I obviously had a bone to pick with the Countess next time we met. Vallodon had kept only ten percent and she had agreed to stick by that rate.

'Well, Mademoiselle Jenny, I think you belong among the *crème de la crème*,' she added quietly. 'Would you care to meet ... the person who has, let us say, inherited the mantle of M Vallodon?'

'And pray, what is his name?' I asked. 'This lucky gentleman who, without once opening his legs, earns almost five thousand francs a week?'

(I've just realized how much my mathematics has improved since I took to this trade; perhaps I have hit upon a novel – not to say lucrative – way to teach arithmetic to young ladies everywhere, in the trade and out?)

'You are quick, mam'selle,' she said approvingly. 'In fact, that lucky proprietor is a woman, a young girl who gave poor Vallodon such a mighty *plaisir* it killed him. She has – er – retired from public life ...'

'In hiding from the police?' I asked excitedly.

'No, no!' She laughed at my naïvete. Either Mme Dutourd was a wonderful actress (which I could not rule out) or she knew far less than I had feared. 'She was pursued by every suicidal hothead in Paris. Offers for one night in her bed ran up to twenty thousand francs. It became absurd.'

I wanted to say, proudly, 'Actually it was pounds sterling.' But was it a trap? 'As for me,' I sighed. 'I am about to be thrown out of the Maison d'Or.'

She tilted her head accusingly. 'D'you mean you really believed all that?'

My astonishment was quite genuine. 'Of course.'

She laughed. 'Well, I must be better at it than I thought. No, Mam'selle Jenny, it was an out-and-out lie. Nothing could have been farther from the truth.'

'But why, madame?' I asked angrily. 'It was a cruel trick – at a time when I was already confused.'

She pacified me with a smile. 'Listen, my dear. Once in every few years, out of the hundreds of girls who pass through our doors ... By the way, we have two new ones coming tomorrow, experienced girls but new here. Blanche and Arlette are going to set up on their own. However, as I was saying – of all those hundreds of girls, once in a long while, we find one who is quite outstanding. When you two came here the other week, I thought your friend Ouné was one. But after only a couple of days I realized it was you.'

'Then why did you ...'

She raised a finger to halt an interruption I *was* about to make. 'I wanted to shock you into realizing your full capabilities. I could see you trying so hard to become like the other girls here. Finding out how *they* coped with the pressure of so much traffic ... trying to work out an attitude to our customers that you could put on like an old hat when you needed it. In short, you were trying to find a way of simply *getting by* – almost as if you were working here for a bet or a dare or something like that.' Her eyes narrowed as she put forward this possibility. 'You're not here for any such reason are you?'

'Oh, no, it's nothing like that, madame.' I now wanted to say as little as possible.

'Because it's quite clear you are not who you claim to be. You have breeding and education. And you have far too much intelligence and wit ever to have been a chambermaid at that hotel – where, incidentally, the manager swears you worked, though none

209

of the staff can remember you at all!' She laughed. 'You should have bribed them all. However – I don't want to pry. All I wish to do is point out to you the possibility of enjoying this same sort of work in much more congenial ways and surroundings – and earning at least ten times as much into the bargain. And the Prefect of Police agrees with me. He knows all those *pouliches* and he says you're the equal of any and far better than most.' She rose and assumed something of her usual frosty manner, dismissing me with the gesture. 'Just think about it, that's all.'

Then, with my hand on the doorknob, she said, 'A small thing, mam'selle – no more cock-sucking, eh?'

I blushed scarlet.

'Not with cadets. If you're uncertain, just glance my way and raise an eyebrow. I'll either nod or look away. Understood?'

'But, madame ... the rules,' I protested.

'Are to be modified by experience.' She smiled.

Friday, 28th May, 1852.
Alors! C'est fini! If I had tried to imagine all the possible ways I might be unmasked, I would never have thought of anything so outlandish as this.

Last night, about ten o'clock, a rather nervous-looking elderly man came into the salon and started searching for someone, a particular girl. It wasn't me, but when he saw me, he must have decided I would do instead. He did not want to sit and cuddle – only to get upstairs and begin. He was sweating and shivery and I asked if he had a fever; but he said no, he'd just been in too much of a hurry. His voice was very low and raspy – which madame said afterwards should have rung an alarm bell within me. It certainly will in future!

Whatever hurrying he had done on his way here, he was quite incapable of repeating indoors; he took an age on the stairs. I kept encouraging him, telling him all the lovely things we could do when he got there; and he told me, a dozen times, I was 'sweet.' But there was no feeling in it – either way, I suppose.

At long last we arrived. I squatted before him and asked him to show me his pego. It was fortunate I was so close, for I saw the knife before he had drawn it out more than half an inch. I leaped back – thwarting his immediate plan, which was to plunge it in my back.

Something within me took over automatically. I don't remember being frightened or my blood running cold or anything like that; there was just an air of absolute unreality to everything – him, me, the room ... everything.

I heard myself give a light laugh. 'Really, m'sieu!' I chided. 'That's no good. You're too late. My last lover has already cut me very deeply. See!' And I lifted my chemise and swept my hands behind me, pulling it tight to show him the tight, hairless cleft of my *cutte*. 'Isn't it deep! Would you like to come a little closer and see how deep?'

It was the last response he had expected, I'm sure. He stood there, looking at me – my face, my cleft, in turn – and shaking his head in bewilderment.

Meanwhile my hands, behind me, were scrabbling for a weapon on the dressing table. I knew I had a paper knife there but could not remember precisely where I'd left it. My finger closed around something long and cold. At first I thought it was the paper knife but then I realized it was only that beautiful, long, thin dildo-douche my grandmother had given me before I came to France.

He recovered and sprang at me with a great roar.

I screamed and, having no other weapon, put my hands in front of me to ward him off – douche and all. The fact that it went right into his open mouth was pure fluke, for I had my eyes shut by now. But I felt my hands jarred as it struck something, and opened my eyes again – only to see it buried, as I supposed, in his throat.

He made a horrible choking sound and raised both hands to his neck. The knife fell to the floor, but my presence of mind had deserted me. I went on standing there, frozen in terror, just holding that douche in his mouth and watching him buckle at the knees and sink to the floor. As soon as he lay at my feet I bolted for the door – just as Mme Dutourd arrived with a pistol.

She was marvellous – as one would expect. There were two officers behind her – stark naked with gleaming wet erections waving in the air, but totally unabashed. One of them took her pistol and held it trained on my unconscious gentleman while the other bent to examine him.

'Dead,' he said laconically.

Madame was crouched at his side in a trice. She pulled that curious silver douche from his mouth, looked at it, and handed it up to me. Its knob was all bent and flattened. 'That'll need some repairs,' she told me. 'Put it away where you won't forget it.' But then she noticed something else and snatched it back. She carried it toward the light and I saw she had recognized the de C. crest and monogram on its base.

The other officer relaxed his vigilance and slowly lowered his gun. 'Shall we get the police?' he asked, looking from Madame to me and back again.

She handed me the douche. 'The Prefect of Police had better be informed,' she said grimly. 'But first we'll let the doctor see what might be done.'

To Geraldine, who was standing in my doorway, she said, 'Send one of the maids for Dr Laland.'

She thanked the two officers and told them they were needed more urgently elsewhere – to warm up two cold and lonely young girls, in fact.

When they had gone, she closed the door and said, 'You had better get dressed, Mademoiselle … what do I call you now?'

'Jenny, Madame,' I replied. 'There is only one person who can tell you any more than that.'

'Yes, indeed! And what is *she* going to say to this?' Her tone was harsh, even accusing.

'You talk as if it were my fault,' I complained.

She moved closer and squeezed my arm reassuringly. 'I'm just up to my old tricks, my dear. I wanted to see if you had crumbled or if there was some fight left in you. I should have guessed.'

'He simply pulled out that knife and came for me. Not a word. Just a great angry bellow.'

'Have you done him before?'

'Never. I'm sure of it. How could that have killed him? There's no blood in his mouth or anything.'

'Did your … grandmother? Is that what she is?'

I nodded.

'Did she send you here?'

'Not to spy. To learn the trade, she said.'

'But inevitably you will carry back tales from here?'

I smiled – I actually smiled – at her. 'Surely you're the last person in the world to be worried at the thought of *that*, Mme Dutourd? If you are, then let me tell you – one of the things I'm going to recommend to my grandmother is a better system of induction and training for girls who are new to the work. They won't all be so fortunate as to begin under a woman like you. So who do you suppose I was going to suggest to organize it? I can truly say it

213

– no one would be better.' Suddenly the absurdity of the situation struck me. 'Why are we talking about this, madame, when there is a dead man at our feet?'

'Because he *is* dead,' she scoffed. 'We get four or five a year, you know. It's nothing very special, this. You wait till August! You were saying?'

'I was only going to add that if by any chance my grandmother doesn't agree – well, just wait until *I* take over the management of the enterprise!'

'Ah! And *that's* why you're working here!'

I thought about it and said, 'That's why I *started* working here.'

The doctor arrived at that moment. He turned the corpse over with his feet and said, 'Ha! I know this fellow. What happened?'

I told him.

'And now you're afraid you may have been the cause of his death, I suppose?'

His dismissive tone made my heart leap up. 'What else can I think, doctor?'

He chuckled. 'No, my dear, this fellow killed himself over forty years ago – when he got himself clapped in the Spanish wars. That's tertiary syphilis for you. He had an aortic aneurysm the size of your thigh. It must have burst as he sprang at you. Your rather charmingly symbolic method of dispatching him had nothing to do with it, I'm afraid. Pity – it would have made an amusing little paper.'

'Nothing at all?' I asked, delighted to hear it.

'Stake my reputation on it.'

'Is he a patient of yours?' Mme Dutourd barked.

He nodded. 'Treated his family for years.'

'The usual, then, I suppose,' she told him.

'Absolutely. No trouble at all. Died in my waiting room. Usual mode of conveyance – a drunk being helped into his carriage? I'll see to it at once.'

Within ten minutes the corpse had gone. The whole episode began to recede. But half an hour later, reality returned with a crash – in the form of my grandmother. She sailed in on an ocean of feathers, pearls, and perfume. Only the sudden arrival of the emperor could have created a greater stir.

'Is this the gel?' she asked, looking directly at me as if she had never seen me before. I curtseyed. 'You poor sweet child!' she went on. 'Come in here where we may be private.'

Mme Dutourd, now knowing who I was, held back but my grandmother motioned her to enter her own parlour, too – as she would if I were any ordinary *poulette*. But as soon as we were private, the Countess unleashed an orgy of subdued commiserations, endearments, and tears.

When she saw how unscathed I was, in fact – both in mind and body – she relaxed. Mme Dutourd poured us each a glass of brandy. 'Is this wise? I shan't be able to go back into the salon after this!' I commented.

They both laughed uproariously and then the whole atmosphere changed.

'So, my darling F-f … Jenny! Your secret is out at last. I think you've done magnificently to have kept it even this long, don't you, Mme Dutourd?'

'She has your blood and breeding, milady. No two ways about it – and M le Comte's, of course.'

The old woman winked at me and murmured, 'One of them, anyway!'

'You admit it?' I asked.

She grinned wickedly.

'And you'd have had me … I mean the things you were planning for …'

Her grin grew even more wicked. 'No one in Paris would have been more disappointed in you than me,

215

if you had stepped off that train at the Gare du Nord, exactly as planned. But I had every confidence you'd make your own journey in that strange, new, and exciting world. The only question is – where has it brought you? What shall you do now?'

It was not, of course, a question to which I had given a great deal of thought since that man fell dead at my feet. In fact, to be perfectly honest, I had given it none at all. So I could only stare at her – hoping, perhaps for suggestions.

'You'll go to your villa now, of course,' she said. 'Have a nice rest … for week or two … buy a few rags … have your portrait painted …' She rattled on in that vein for a while and then peered at me to see whether I had gone to sleep with my eyes open. 'I was rather hoping for a response of some kind.'

I sighed. 'I don't think I want to do just *nothing*. I feel I want to keep busy at something.'

She raised an approving eyebrow. 'Come and stay with me then? Sit at my right hand and see how the business is organized, day by day?'

'That would be very good,' Mme Dutourd chimed in, giving me an encouraging nod.

'All right,' I said brightly.

'Go and get your hat and coat – and any little thing you might need immediately – there's a dear. You can ride home with me.'

I had reached the door when she said – purely as a matter of form – to Mme Dutourd, 'You can manage without her tonight, of course.'

And, of course, madame assured her she could.

And then I thought of that salon – the soft lighting, the gentle, smiling, sweet-smelling girls, the excitement in the men's eyes … the chatter, the endless movement … the novelty and the reassuring sameness of it all … the unending parade of nude men in their thousands of varieties ... the urgency of their desire ...

I thought of Victor and Paul ... of Jeannette and Célestine, whose lives had lasted one glorious hour ... of M d'Alembert, who stalked our pleasure like a big-game hunter ... of the boudoir, and the aroma of powder and perfume and young girls' bodies ... of Blanche and Arlette, now gone, yet still remembered ... of Desirée and Lalage, the two new girls, whose stories I had only half heard ... of Jacqui, transformed by her discovery of the dark, primal powers lurking within her ... of Geraldine, so pretty, so down-to-earth, such good company ... and of Ouné! How could I even think of leaving my lovely Ouné? Or any of them?

'Hurry up, my dear!' my grandmother chided.

'D'you know, Countess,' I said, turning back to them both. 'I think I'd actually prefer to stay here and carry on as before – with Mme Dutourd's connivance, of course.'

My grandmother turned pale; her jaw fell open; for a moment I thought she was going to scream abuse at me. But then the most seraphic smile I ever saw split her face – almost cutting it in two. 'Now!' she crowed. 'Oh, Mme Dutourd! Do you hear her? Is she not a true de C? To the very core of her being.' And she burst into tears and hugged me and told me I'd made her so proud.

'Only for a year or two,' I added. 'Or three. Then I'm sure something else new and exciting will turn up. It always does.'

I did four more customers after that and went to bed wondering how a day so full of alarms and excursions could feel as if it were the happiest of my life.

Then I realized I had forgotten to raise the matter of my grandmother's keeping twenty percent of the earnings of the *crème de la crème*.

But suddenly it didn't seem to matter any more. Ten percent ... twenty percent ... what was the difference? After all, working here, I keep only fifty percent – and I'm perfectly happy.

Yes, *perfectly* happy.